Chronic
A Sick Novel

Paul Lima

Chronic
A *Sick* Novel

Paul Lima

This book is dedicated to my wife Lyn who has been with me in sickness and in health, but for the last seven years mostly in sickness.

This book is also dedicated to MS Warriors everywhere, to other chronically ill folks, and to those with any malady that knocks them off their feet.

"What defines us is how well we rise after falling." - Unknown

Thanks to Kathleen Hamilton and Jeannette Terrell for their proofreading assistance.

Special thanks to Gabriele Pulpan for her vigorous copyediting and for her insightful comments that helped me tighten the writing and bring greater focus to the book. It is a better book because of her.

Note: I made edits after the book was proofread, so any typos are all mine! If you spot a typo, or want to comment on the book, email paulmslima@gmail.com.

Chronic
- First Edition 2020

Cover and interior design: Paul Lima. Copyright © 2020

Published by Paul Lima Presents
www.paullima.com/books

ISBN: 978-1-927710-47-0

Contents

Chapter One

Paul Amil is dreaming that he is packing. His suitcase is small and full and he is still trying to cram in clothes, shoes, cans of food, a loaf of bread, and toilet paper. His dream location alters and he is driving a truck, suitcase in his lap as he reaches over it to shift gears. It is pouring rain. His windshield wipers work, but only intermittently. The road is narrow and rocky. His headlights illuminate a sign: "Road Ends." What he can see, when the wipers clear his window, is the end of the road, which drops off steeply. He hits the breaks but the truck skids over a cliff. As he spills over in slow motion, he wakes up with a jolt and in a sweat. He opens his eyes and sees his hands in front of him, reaching out to break his fall.

*   *   *

Paul, who has just turned thirty-five, has some indigenous blood in him. This gives his skin a slightly shaded hue. He has high cheek bones, inherited from his Native grandfather, and his thin eyelashes blink inquiringly over large, dark eyes. His long nose slops gently down to just above thin red lips. For a decade, he had relapsing remitting multiple sclerosis. His symptoms-- various aches, pains, tingles, and eye issues--would come and go, lasting for several weeks, and often for several months or longer. Then they would disappear and he'd feel fine for a month or more, until the next MS exacerbation. However, he does not have secondary progressive MS with symptoms that come and do not go. Nor does he have primary progressive MS. People with PPMS progress at different speeds but they all move from walking with canes, to riding scooters, to requiring wheelchairs. Some hit the point where they are unable to get out of bed without assistance.

1

Chronic

Paul blames his white genes for his MS, as it is a rare disease amongst indigenous people. His blame is ironic because his mother was a short, strong, healthy Italian-Canadian. She was killed in her late fifties while riding her motorcycle. When Paul was thirty, she was hit by a truck making an illegal left turn. His father, slightly overweight, half Native American and half white, died from a heart attack hours after hearing about the death of his wife. It was as if he could not live without her and wanted to join her, he loved her that much, Paul thought.

Paul looks at the clock on his night table. It is seven-thirty a.m. He has time to shower and have breakfast before he meets with Deena Troy, a woman in her mid-thirties with Parkinson's disease. They became friends over several renovations that Deena completed at his house, his old house that he no longer shares with Quelina Applebee, his indigenous ex-wife who still lives there. He left her because of his MS, telling her she should meet someone new, and healthy, and get on with life.

Quelina is a therapist. She didn't understand why Paul, a motivational speaker--or former motivational speaker, as he now describes himself--left. As hard as she tried, using every therapeutic trick in the book, she could not talk him out of leaving. So she let him go, understanding that letting him leave was what he needed to accept, or at least better deal with, a disease that was destroying his ability to be the man he wanted to be.

Paul uses a cane to walk. He can amble without it, but his balance is often shaky. He has various body pains and suffers intermittent fatigue that can be so profound that it causes him to pass out. That is why he describes himself as a former motivational speaker. He no longer wants to take to the stage, fearing he might be hit by an attack of fatigue and pass out while speaking. "Not very motivational," he told Quelina before leaving.

His website says he is on temporary hiatus from motivational speaking. It is as if he cannot accept that his speaking days are over, that he hopes his condition will magically improve.

Paul and Deena are looking to rent a flat in the west end of Toronto. Deena is a tall, dark-haired Canadian of Greek descent,

2

with bright round eyes, an aquiline nose, and lips that seem to fill the lower half of her face. A renovator by trade, she has had Parkinson's disease for a decade and it's slowly getting worse-- making it difficult for her to swallow at times, giving her irritating skin issues, and causing her, especially her arms and hands, to shake.

Shakes are not a good thing for a renovator, not when there is wood to saw, screws to turn, and nails to hammer. She can still drive and haul supplies and equipment around job sites, but the finer side of her work is becoming more difficult, although not yet impossible, to do.

Deena's partner, Gilbert Lion, still lives with her and their son, Reggie. But he emotionally fled the relationship as Deena's Parkinson's progressed. Gilbert could not deal with the increased shaking and diminished sexual libido that the disease caused. When Paul moved into temporary quarters--"slum quarters," he calls the room he lives in--she asked him if he wanted to pool their resources and find a flat to rent because she and Gilbert were breaking up. "I love Reggie to pieces, but he should stay with a healthy dad, so he and Gilbert will keep the apartment.

*   *   *

Deena and Paul are at the door of a house on Indian Road near Garden Avenue. They found the "flat for rent" posting on Kijiji, a classified ad website. The house is owned by Martha Nichol, an interior designer who renovated the three-bedroom first floor of the house for her husband Mike, who had primary progressive MS.

Mike valiantly fought his MS with humour, MS drugs, and the occasional beer, as he moved from cane to scooter to wheelchair to being unable to get out of bed. He died from respiratory complications caused by his increasing inability to move much and stretch out his lungs.

Martha had renovated the first floor in an open concept style, with lower counters, drawers, cupboards, and appliances and a fully accessible washroom so that Mike could be as self-sufficient as possible while dealing with his PPMS. Martha now lives on the second and third floors of the house with her daughter Genevieve, a first-year English major at the University of Toronto.

While Paul and Deena are not in wheelchairs, and hope not to be for a long time, if ever, they are looking for a flat that will accommodate them should their diseases progress to such a state.

Paul leans on his cane and rings the doorbell. Martha, dressed in an embroidered long-sleeved blouse, floor-length skirt, and well-worn army boots, answers the door. Her face is not young, but not yet old. She has large, bright-green eyes and a great deal of wildly curly brunette and grey hair which is loosely tied back with a red ribbon. She greets Paul and Deena with warm hellos, waves them in, and takes them on a tour of the flat. Much of Mike's furniture has remained in the wheelchair-friendly apartment and is available if they rent the unit, which Paul and Deena appreciate. They also like the easily accessible counters and cupboards and the bathroom equipped with various grab bars.

"If we rent the flat, we hope we never need all that you've done here," Paul says to Martha. "But you never know."

"My husband, Mike, found it comforting to be able to cope on his own when our daughter and I were out, or I just needed some time to hide away," Martha says.

Deena inspects the various renovations to the flat. "You had good people working on this job," she says.

"I did the design work and Harold Reckon was the contractor. He put a good team together."

"I'll have to ask him why he didn't call me," Deena says with a laugh.

"You do renovation work?" Martha asks.

"Harold is one of my primary contractors."

"If you take the place and we need any other renovations, I guess I won't have to call Harold," Martha laughs. "I guess we should discuss rent," she continues. "It includes the fridge, stove, microwave, use of laundry facilities in the basement, and any of the furniture you see here--kitchen table and chairs, couch and living room chairs, the flat-screen TV, chests of drawers in the three bedrooms. In addition, access to the Internet via Wi-Fi, as well as heat, water, and utilities are included. Basically, all you'd need are beds."

"That is very useful," says Paul, "because other than my clothes a bed is about the only thing I have."

"My ex and son need our furniture, so this place is great," adds Deena.

Martha tells them the monthly rental amount she is seeking. They ask her to give them a moment to discuss it. Martha goes into the kitchen. A few minutes later Deena and Paul join her, with cheerless looks on their faces.

"We love what you've done with the place, and all that's included. No denying that it would be ideal for us," Paul says.

"We think the rent makes sense for the neighborhood and for this place, a renovated three-bedroom," Deena continues.

"Unfortunately," says Paul, "it's a tad steep for us. I think we're going to have to look for a smaller flat that hasn't been renovated in the manner that you've done here."

"Again, it is an excellent reno," says Deena.

Martha nods understandingly. "It's unfortunate that people with disabilities tend to have limited incomes. They're on pensions or restricted in the work they can do. At the same time, I can't afford to lower the rent or re-renovate the flat to bring it back to, shall we say, able-bodied standards. It's like we're all between a rock and a hard place."

"Not a comfortable place to be, but here we are," says Paul.

The door to the flat opens and a lanky girl with a disarming smile steps in. "Hope I'm not interfering with anything," says Genevieve. "Just wanted to tell mom that I'm off to class." Her jet-black hair, shaved at the sides and cropped short at the back, has loopy curls on top, a couple of which fall over her eyes. She brushes them back as she chats.

Martha introduces Genevieve to Paul and Deena. "They've just finished looking at the place. Unfortunately, we don't have a match between the rent we need and what they can afford."

"That's unfortunate. If I had a job, I'd take the third bedroom and we could spit the rent thee ways," she laughs.

Paul looks at Deena who looks at Martha. "Do we have light bulbs shining above our heads?" Martha asks.

"I wouldn't object to a third roommate," says Paul.

"I'd be okay with that too," says Deena.

"I have other people coming to look at the place," says Martha. "It's a long shot, but maybe somebody else will need roommates. If you can hang out for a while, come upstairs for tea, we'll see how it goes."

"We're in," says Paul.

"I'll put the kettle on," says Martha.

"Cool," says Genevieve. "Glad I was able to help."

*   *   *

A short while later, Martha, Paul, and Deena are in the upstairs kitchen drinking tea and discussing how they might approach potential tenants with their idea of sharing the flat when the doorbell rings. Martha had been expecting Bolton Lewis fifteen minutes earlier, she explained to Paul and Deena, but nobody showed. "I presume Bolton had a change of plans or found a place. That should be Albert Booth," she says as she heads downstairs to answer the door.

When she opens the door, she sees two people in front of her. A black man in his early twenties in a manual wheelchair had wheeled up the front ramp that her husband had used. Beside him is a tall, broad-shouldered white man in his late thirties with a smoothly shaved head.

"I'm sorry that I'm late," says Bolton, the man in the wheelchair. He runs a hand through the tight curls of his short dark hair. "Wheel-Trans was late picking me up. When I tried to call you, I discovered that my phone battery was dead."

"He can view the apartment first," says Albert, with a deep voice. "I'm in no rush."

"Why don't we save time? You can both come in and look around," says Martha. Albert and Bolton look at each other and nod. They enter the house and Martha takes them on a tour of the flat. They poke around in each room. Albert asks questions about the renovations. Martha tells them that the flat was designed for her husband. Bolton is mostly silent.

"I did renovations on my house. Nothing this extensive, but I enjoyed the work. I guess you can call me an amateur fixer-upper," says Albert.

"You mentioned on the phone that you were taking some time off work," Martha says to Albert. "If you don't mind my asking, why would that be?"

"I've got hockey cancer," says Albert. "Non-Hodgkin lymphoma, also known as NHL. It's a cancer that starts in the white blood cells. I then developed lung cancer. Although I'm in remission now, I'm not cancer-free. Some microscopic cancer remains, but I'll take remission over full-blown cancer any day. I'm on long-term disability. I am, or was, a nurse at Saint Michael's Hospital."

"My husband Mike knew that hospital well," says Martha. "The MS Clinic is at Saint Mike's."

"That's right," says Albert. "I worked on the cardiology ward."

Martha clears her throat. "And what put you in a wheelchair?" she asks Bolton.

"Car accident," he says in a subdued tone. His legs, which in a Toronto Star article about up-and-coming amateur sprinters, had once been compared to the trunks of majestic oak trees, were now skinny twigs wrapped in soft cotton track pants, one of the few materials that didn't feel uncomfortable on him.

Martha picks up on his tone and doesn't ask for details about the accident.

As they are touring the flat, Martha tells them all that is included in the rent. When the tour is over, she claps her hands together. "Any questions before I tell you the amount I'm asking for to rent the flat."

Albert and Bolton shake their heads and she lets them know the monthly rental fee.

Bolton is the first to speak. "It's much too high. I knew that it would be when I wheeled in through the door. For some reason, I thought I'd be looking at a one-bedroom flat, the kind that is often available in this area. I must have misread the ad."

"Or it wasn't clear," Martha laughs. "Depends on where you read it. Some online ad sites restricted word count, unless you pay extra. If my cheapness was the cause of any confusion, I'm sorry about that."

Bolton laughs and Albert says, "I knew it was a full flat, but didn't know it would be this nice or have three bedrooms and such great renovation work. Sadly, it's too expensive for me too. Worth it, but too expensive."

"Well," says Martha, "what if I said I have two people interested in the flat who also can't quite afford it? If one of you took one room and shared the flat with them, the rent would be a third of what I just said."

Albert rubs his chin. "That brings it closer to what I was looking to spend."

"That's still a bit high for me," says Bolton. "I really should have wheeled away at the door. I'll just call Wheel-Trans, if I can borrow a phone that does not have a dead battery. They should be here in thirty minutes or so."

"You're more than welcome to wait here," says Martha. "Why don't I go upstairs and get Paul and Deena. Albert, you can meet them and talk things over." With that, Martha heads upstairs.

Albert lends Bolton his cell phone, and says, "Before you call Wheel-Trans, let me ask you something."

Bolton nods.

"What if your rent was half of a third?"

"Glad I have a business degree," laughs Bolton. "Let me do the math" He pauses for a moment, calculating. "That would work. But there's only one spare bedroom."

"But what if it was the master bedroom and we had two single beds in it? One bedroom means one-third of the rent, sharing it would reduce that by half." Albert pauses as he watches Bolton ruminating.

"You'd want a roommate?" Bolton asks

"It would work for me. And, between us, I could use a further cut in the rent."

"The price would be right, but shouldn't we first talk about, I don't know, the implications of sharing a room."

"If you mean nudity when we're putting on our pajamas, let me reassure you that as a nurse I've seen a lot of naked people." Bolton laughs as Albert continues. "Also, although I am, or was, your stereotypical gay male nurse, since my cancer, I've hung up my sexual spurs. Chemo takes it out of me. So sex is not an issue."

"It's not an issue for me either because…" Bolton hesitates. "I don't function that way anymore. A car crash can take it out of you." He pauses. "Tell you what, let's see how the others react to the idea, and then we can all talk it over."

Albert nods as Martha, Paul, and Deena come into the flat. Martha does the introductions and everybody bumps elbows, the new way of shaking hands that caught on during the Coronavirus pandemic, and stayed that way as the pandemic was all but put to rest with the development of vaccines.

"Do you folks want to discuss the possibility of sharing the flat?" asks Martha. "Three bedrooms means the rent would be split three ways. If that works for three of you, then it works for me."

Albert clears his throat. "Bolton and I haven't talked this completely through, but would you two be willing to take on two roommates? We could share the master bedroom, if that was not an issue, and split one-third of the rent. The additional split would put the rent in the ballpark that we can both afford."

Paul looks at Deena who shrugs her shoulders. "It means we wouldn't have to fight over which of us gets the master bedroom," he says to her.

"Martha, would you be okay with that?" Deena asks.

"I don't want to say the more the merrier, but if it works for the four of you…"

Albert says to Bolton, "The master bedroom is a decent size and has a nice closet and chest of drawers. Single beds at either side of the room would work for me."

Bolton takes a breath. "Albert and I discussed the elephant in the room…"

"Which is?" asks Paul.

"Sex, or other relationships," says Bolton.

Chronic

"I was a male nurse," says Albert with a short, rueful laugh. "I had just started living with Leon Frijol, an orderly at Saint Mike's, the hospital I worked at. But we're not together any longer because cancer has put an end to my libido, so no worries about me bringing anyone home."

"I know Saint Mike's. I go to the MS clinic there," says Paul.

Albert and Martha nod and Albert continues, "Leon and I had literally just moved in together when I was diagnosed. We've agreed to go our separate ways." Albert pauses as if he is trying to swallow a lump in his throat. "So there is no elephant in the room for me."

"There is no elephant in the room for me either," says Bolton. He sighs. "The car accident that I was involved in put me in this chair and ended my sexual escapades. I had a girlfriend, a hairdresser who makes candles on the side. We're still friends, but only because she's crazy, in a good way." Bolton pauses, as he too is becoming emotional. "We still chat. But sex is not on the table for me anymore."

"Ah, I remember sex on the table," Paul laughs. "I have MS and one of my symptoms is a constant testicular numbness, as if my testicles have fallen asleep. That coupled with my fatigue and a couple of other issues have zapped my sexual desire." Paul pauses for a moment as if reminiscing, and then continues, "I told my wife, my ex-wife, that she should get on with her life without me. She resisted at first, but I told her she was way too young for what MS was doing to us. I hugged her and we had a good cry about it. We've split up but are still friends."

"Just to complete the trifecta, or quatrafecta, or whatever you'd call a four-person run," Deena says with an ironic grin, "Parkinson's disease, which I have, is caused by a loss of nerve cells in a part of the brain that is responsible for producing dopamine, which is involved in sexual activity. I have no sexual desire, which is one of the reasons why my ex and I split up. He wanted out and bluntly told me so. There were some other issues before I was diagnosed and my illness became the perfect excuse to end the relationship." Deena looks around at the assembled group.

"I guess that makes this an asexual household," says Martha. "Since we're all being honest, for me it has to do with getting older and, I confess, once Mike lost the ability to function that way my desire to do so just kind of evaporated. I'd rather focus on my interior design and volunteer work at a women's shelter, and reading and crocheting."

"If you don't mind my asking," says Deena, "what about your daughter Genevieve? I remember being her age and healthy. I had a rather vigorous sexual appetite."

In response, everybody, even Martha, laughs. Then Martha says, "You folks seem like the type who have open minds, so I'll tell you, and I know Genevieve won't mind because she's open about it." Martha pauses for a moment, as if rethinking what she is about to say, but then says it. "Genevieve is *they*. They are non-binary."

"That doesn't mean no sex though," says Albert.

"For the moment it does," says Martha, "because they are trying to figure out, based on birth gender, if they are heterosexual or homosexual. I know it sounds weird, but they are working it all out. Also, they seem to prefer to read and study. In other words, they spend the time they would be engaged in sexual escapades reading books and writing essays for school."

Paul laughs. "There are only twenty-four hours in the day and I have more time for my art, now that I'm not having sex," he says. "I'm not saying sex is a waste of time, but you can get a lot more done with your limited time on earth if you are not spending it screwing around."

Everybody laughs at that and then Deena says, "Being sick and caring for yourself eats up the time one would have spent on sex. In addition to no desire, I don't have time for sex."

"Amen to that," says Albert.

"Waiting for Wheel-Trans to pick you up and get you to wherever you need to go also eats up a lot of time," says Bolton. "Not equating Wheel-Trans with sex, but using it eats into the time you have, even if you have next to nothing to spend time on."

"We live in an overly sexualized society," says Deena. "Not being sexually active doesn't mean that your life has come to an end."

"In some ways," says Martha, "it feels like it has come to a new beginning."

"Cheers to that," says Paul.

"But there are days I miss it," says Bolton. "I think what I miss more than anything is the exhaustion. The exhaustion from having a great workout, a great race, or a great bout of sex."

Everybody nods in tacit agreement, and then Paul says, "Then what you need to replace your sexual exhaustion is MS fatigue. Knocks you out without expending any energy at all."

"This is all so familiar," says Martha, "Mike had primary progressive MS, the worst kind, and it took him. When shit like that happens, it changes your priorities."

"So true," says Paul.

Bolton looks at his watch. "I'm not trying to rush things, but I need to give Wheel-Trans thirty minutes notice, so I was wondering what the next step is."

"Your wheelchair will fit in the back of my van," says Deena. "Happy to give you a lift home."

Bolton nods in thanks and Martha says, "Bolton is right though. We should figure out the next steps. The first thing that I have to ask, for your safety as much as mine, is has everybody had their coronavirus vaccines?"

The four potential tenants flex their right arms in what has become the universal coronavirus vaccine salute.

"Good to see," says Martha, flexing her right arm back. "I'm not a very formal person. In theory, I should do credit checks, but why don't you each tell me what you do and how you can afford to pay your rent? It has to add up for each of you if you are going to be roommates, as well as for me as landlord. If it does, then we'll talk about what happens next."

"I can start," says Deena. "I'm separating and leaving our apartment, but get to keep the van that I use to haul supplies to renovation jobs. For how long I can work, I don't know. I can carry heavy material, but it's getting difficult to control this Parkinson's shaking, making the more refined work--sawing, hammering or, no pun intended, screwing, more difficult. However, my son Reggie is taking time off school--he's only sixteen but says he's ready for a scholastic break. He helps me on various jobs to make some cash. And I have a solid chunk of change in the bank."

Martha nods appreciatively. "Sounds good. Albert?"

"I'm in remission from my cancer, but still get treatments to help keep me there. I'm on extended sick leave, which means I have a monthly disability income. And hey, Deena, if you ever need somebody to help you saw, hammer or, as you say, no pun intended, screw, I'd be happy to work with you. I have experience putting stuff together. You can be my eyes and I can be your hands, so to speak."

"You know, Reggie is going camping with some friends in a couple of weeks so I just might take you up on that," says Deena. "If it works out, I'd try to land larger jobs so that there will be even more work."

"With or without the renovation work, which would be nice to do if I'm up to your standards, I'm good for half of a third of the rent," says Albert.

"Two down," says Martha. "Paul?"

"I used to be a motivational speaker," Paul says. "If you look at my website, which is still up, it says I'm taking time off. Can you see me halfway through a talk, telling my audience that they will have to take a break because I'm going to pass out from fatigue? I guess a part of me was hoping that I'd go into remission and would be able to resume my speaking." He pauses and shakes his head as if trying to clear cobwebs that have descended upon him. "Anyway, I'm into painting now-- pictures, not houses--which makes me no money. I get along with my ex. If she sells the house, I'd have a large chunk of change coming to me. I don't need her to make a move yet... Paul hesitates and clears his throat. "...because I also do some freelance writing for corporate clients. The work is done from home and they don't see me pass out from fatigue. I have several clients using me now and then. Considering all that is included in the rent and that we'd divide the rent three ways, I'm comfortable with my share."

"Sounds good," says Martha. "Bolton?"

Bolton turns to Albert. "You said you were a stereotype, a gay male nurse. However, you are not the only stereotype. I was a sprinter before the accident. Black sprinters? Bet you've never heard of them before." He grins as the others laugh. "I had hoped to try out for Canada's Olympic team, but..." He pauses. "I have a business degree, did website design and social media promotion for a company before my accident, and confess that I am now between jobs. I have modest savings and am keeping my head above water as I look for work."

"Just curious," says Deena, "don't you have an accident insurance settlement?"

Bolton wheels his wheelchair back and forth for a moment. "You don't get insurance money when..." He hesitates and then inhales. "...you caused the accident."

"Sorry," says Deena. "I didn't mean to pry."

"Not a problem," says Bolton. "You folks need to know the truth about me." He wipes his nose with the back of his hand. "I lost the last race of the indoor season. It was close, but I was second, which is a loss. A group of us went to a pub after the race. I had a bit too much to drink..." He hesitates. "And did cocaine. Then drove home."

"And?" says Paul in a quiet voice.

"And I caused the accident that put me in this chair. It was only me and a telephone pole. Nobody else was injured, thank goodness. It's been nine months. I haven't had any alcohol since, and haven't even thought of touching cocaine or had the desire to do so. I'm clean and sober and looking for work. And I can pay my share of the rent if it's half of a third. I don't know what we're going to do for food, but I can contribute to groceries too."

"Thanks," says Paul. "Martha?"

"It all works for me," she says.

"Roommate!" says Albert. He leans over and gives Bolton a post-pandemic air hug.

All four folks stand around silently for a minute, absorbing the implications of each other's maladies and the decision they have just made. The fact that they are each about to embark on a new leg of their journey is descending upon them in a huge wave.

Breaking the ice, Martha gets back to business and says, "If we are all in agreement, the place is empty now. You folks can move in anytime. Rent won't come due until the first of the month so the next two weeks are on the house. Time to get organized, move in, and settle down."

Paul, Deena, Albert, and Bolton look at each other and smile. "So we have an agreement?" asks Paul. "Deena and I each pay a third of the rent. You two split a third. And we can work out the details in terms of grocery shopping, cooking, and cleaning once we're all in."

"Which for me would be some time this weekend," says Bolton. "My landlord is renovating and asked me to leave last month so he can get started. All I have is a few pots, dishes, cutlery, and clothes to move. And a single bed. I can call an Uber to help me move."

"Nonsense," says Deena. "Not while I have a van. Hell, I have so little to move beyond clothes, I can probably get all our stuff in the van in one trip. I'm going to miss living with my son, but I see him on jobs, and I won't have to see my ex, so the sooner the better for me. This weekend it is."

"I'd love to leave the temporary hell hole I'm in now," says Paul. "I pay weekly and can give notice at any time. I can move everything that I have in the car my ex has. I have to buy a bed and can have them deliver it here. If I go bed-shopping when we leave, I can make it this weekend too."

"I too have to buy a bed so that Gilbert can move off the couch back into the bedroom," says Deena with a laugh. "This weekend works for me."

"We have another trifecta of four," says Albert. "My ex and I gave notice. He can keep the apartment until the end of the month. I'm ready to rock and roll, so this weekend works for me too."

"I'm here this weekend to lend a hand," says Martha "as is Genevieve. Sounds like it's all hands on deck."

Chapter Two

Paul Amil is dreaming of boiling a large pot of rice. A huge amount of rice spills out of the pot, runs down the stove, spills on to the floor, and envelops Paul. He is drowning in flowing rice. He feels like he is in a Woody Allen movie, the one in which Woody is chased by instant pudding spilling out of a pot on the stove. He punches at the rice, breaks free of it, and races away. He wakes up in a jolt and a sweat, not able to recall the name of the Woody Allen movie...

*   *   *

It's Saturday. Moving day. Deena and Bolton are the first to arrive in Deena's van, with Bolton's bed and several bags and boxes tucked in the cargo bay. Bolton's wheelchair is folded up beside his bed. Bolton, in the passenger seat, also a box on his lap.

Deena parks in the driveway and hauls Bolton's wheelchair out of the back of the van. She pushes it beside the van's passenger door and helps Bolton in, pretty much lifting him.

"Muscles you have," says Bolton.

"They come in handy on the job," says Deena.

Bolton, his lap full of bags, wheels towards the front door, which Genevieve opens. "Come on in they call!" They offer a post-pandemic air shake and a smile. He thanks them for opening the door and heads in as they head toward the van to help Deena who is hauling the bed out.

Martha comes through the front door to lend a hand with bags and boxes as Bolton wheels back out to get more stuff. "Load my lap up," he says to Martha as Genevieve and Deena trundle by with the bed.

As they continue to move various bags and boxes, Paul and Quelina, a statuesque woman with intense dark eyes and long black hair in a ponytail, show up in Quelina's car. She is wearing a loose-fitting blue blouse and faded designer jeans.

Paul introduces Quelina to his new roommates and to his landlord and her daughter. "We don't have a heck of a lot to move in," he says. "My bed should be delivered later this morning.

As Quelina empties the trunk of her car of a few bags, Santali Lewis shows up in a small red sports car with rusted fenders. "Is this the house Bolton is moving into?" she asks Paul.

Santali, from Bangladesh, is a bit younger than Bolton and about the height Bolton would be if he could stand. She has long, kinky auburn hair that cascades over her shoulders and is wearing patched jeans and a red blouse with short sleeves that expose wiry arms and a fit figure.

"He should be out for another load in a moment," Paul says as, almost magically, Bolton wheels his way out of the house.

"I see you've met Santali," Bolton says to Paul, who introduces Quelina to him and Santali.

Santali bends down and greets Bolton with an air hug. "What can I do?" she asks.

"I think we may be suffering from too many hands," replies Bolton. As if his statement is prescient, Albert shows up in an Uber.

"I have a few things in the back and in the trunk. My bed should be arriving shortly," Albert says.

Bolton introduces Albert to Santali and Paul introduces Quelina to him. Bolton says to Santali, "Fill my lap with bags from the van. Carry in a box or two, and we'll make short work of unloading!"

"Can I help?" asks a young teen who walks up to the house.

"And you are?" asks Paul with a smile.

"Reggie Troy-Fromm, Deena's son. I told mom I was free today to help move stuff." Reggie is a compact, clean-cut sixteen-year-old, with precise features that one might expect to find on a more mature person. He has longish soft blonde hair and inquisitive deep brown eyes.

Deena comes out of the house and waves hello to her son. They elbow bump. "Pick up anything you see and move it in," she says, waving at Albert who is lugging several boxes towards the front door as Deena says hello to Quelina and Santali.

All the bags and boxes are soon moved in and the beds arrive. Once they are in place, the move is complete, other than some leftover unpacking of several boxes in the kitchen.

*　　*　　*

The new roommates and their helpers are sitting around the living room, making full use of the couch, living room chairs, and kitchen chairs that they hauled into the living room.

"Many hands make light work," says Paul, leaning on his cane.

"We still have to sort out the kitchen," says Deena. "I think we have a few redundancies."

"Extra stuff you can store in the basement until you decide what you want to do with it," says Martha. "I've shifted some things around and you will see there is plenty of space for storage."

"Would anybody like a drink?" asks Genevieve. "We figured you'd be short on groceries today, so we put some pop and juice in the fridge."

"And the food is on us," adds Martha, "We're not cooking for you, but ordering pizza, if that suits everybody."

"That is so thoughtful of you," says Deena.

"I think I know which box my glasses and napkins are in," says Albert with a chuckle.

"And I have some cutlery," chimes in Paul.

"You cut pizza and eat it with a fork?" asks Deena, to much laughter.

"Who wants what on their pizza?" asks Martha. "Or who does not want what?"

"Anything is fine by me, other than anchovies," says Bolton. "Oh, and no pineapple."

"Can we make that unanimous?" asks Paul, to which everybody nods in agreement. Then he tells folks he needs to go rest while they are waiting for the pizza. "If I'm not out of my room when it gets here, dig in and don't bother knocking on my door. But save me a couple of slices."

"Are you okay?" asks Quelina.

"You know the drill," Paul replies. "It's been a big day and I can feel the fatigue coming on. If I'm not back after you eat, take off guilt free!" He leans over and gives her an air-peck, then heads to his room.

*   *   *

When Paul ambles out of his bedroom, Martha and Genevieve have gone upstairs and the rest of the helpers have left. Nobody is in the living room because his roommates have all gone to their rooms to make beds and put clothes away. They have agreed to meet back in the living room after straightening up to discuss living arrangements in greater detail.

Paul opens the fridge and finds some slices of pizza wrapped in tin foil on a plate. "Ah, dinner," he sighs, unwrapping two slices and placing them in the microwave for a minute. While they are warming up, he pours himself a glass of ginger ale. When the microwave beeps, he gets his plate, moves to the living room couch, and places his plate and soda on the coffee table in preparation to chow down.

Paul is sitting on the couch finishing his pizza when Albert and Bolton come out of their shared room and grab living room chairs.

"Welcome back," says Albert.

"Fatigue," says Paul. "When it hits, it hits. Not much I can do about it other than go crash and black out. Thanks for the pizza. It was good. So happy to not have to cook tonight."

"I get tired and have to lie down," says Albert, "but nothing like what you are describing."

"We all have our crosses to bear," says Paul. Then he asks, "So, what have folks been up to?"

"Arranging our room. It's going to work well," says Albert.

"We have lots of room between the beds and the closet is big enough for the clothes we need to hang up," says Bolton. "And

Albert and I are splitting the chest of drawers in the room. He's got two drawers and I'm taking one for my socks, t-shirts, and stuff. That way I don't have to keep them in a box under my bed."

Deena joins them, sitting on the couch next to Paul. She looks at the empty plate on the coffee table and says, "I see somebody found the pizza."

Paul laughs.

"Ready to rumble?" she says.

"What are we doing?" asks Paul.

"Sorting out living arrangement details," answers Albert. "If you are up to a chat."

"I don't know that there is much to sort out," says Paul. "We can hide in our rooms and only come out to eat once in a while."

"And use the bathroom," adds Bolton.

"Agreed," says Deena. "Still, I guess we need to decide if we're going to eat any meals together and if so, who buys what."

"And arrange a who-cleans-what-when schedule," says Albert.

"Parking is not an issue," says Deena, "as I'm the only one with a vehicle. I told Martha I'd be happy to pay for street parking, but she said there is room beside her car in the back, which is where my van is now."

"And a TV-watching schedule," says Paul. "Who gets which nights to choose what we watch, if we watch. Although we only have a basic cable package so I don't know that there will be much to choose from."

"Cable?" says Bolton. "I download programs. I'm into British TV series. Watch them on my laptop. If anybody is interested in my downloads or has any requests, I'm happy to search for stuff and hook up my laptop to the flat screen Martha left for us. We can watch together."

"Cool," says Deena. "Happy to discover new shows. I am getting tired of *The Big Bang Theory* and *Law and Order* reruns."

"Okay," summarizes Paul, "food, cleaning, and TV. I think we can sort that all out."

And that is what they do, they figure out who cleans what and when, and who cooks and when. And they create a grocery pool, giving Bolton a break on how much he has to contribute.

"You guys are so, I don't know, generous," Bolton says. "When money starts coming in, I'll pull my full weight. Promise."

"When you're sick you have little else to do, other than be nice," says Albert.

"I don't know," says Paul. "I've been to some MS support meetings and have seen some angry sick people. Not many, but they are out there. Not that I blame them!"

"Don't get me wrong," says Albert. "I'm freaking angry, about my cancer. But take it out on others? What's the point?"

"I agree," says Deena. "My Parkinson's is my condition. It has nothing to do with any of you. I'll hide in my room and punch my pillow some nights when feeling down, but there is no point in sabotaging what has the potential to be a great living arrangement."

"When I act like an ass," says Bolton with a laugh, "you all have the right to tell me to piss off." He pauses and then says, "I'll try my best to learn from you folks. Love your collective attitude and approach to life. Seriously. This feels like what I've needed."

"Just so you know, Bolton," says Paul. "I too have my asshole moments. But like Deena, I work hard to make them my moments, not shared moments."

"Amen to that," says Deena. "Attitude doesn't make you better, but it does make a difference in how you live your life."

"Agreed," Albert laughs. "For instance, meditation won't heal you but it can help you adjust your outlook and how you cope with your illness. And with that, I'm going to meditate for a bit and then crash."

"Will I disturb you later when I come to bed?" asks Bolton.

"Not at all. I'm a sound sleeper, so hit the sack whenever you want. Don't worry about making noise or turning on lights. I'll be fine."

*   *   *

The next morning the roommates are all in the kitchen at the same time. Paul, Deena, and Bolton are at loose ends. Albert is pulling a can of ground coffee out of the cupboard. "I bought this before moving in. Would anybody like a cup?"

"Oh, thank goodness," says Deena. "I thought I'd have to go to Tim Hortons for a coffee."

"And I have eggs and bread in the fridge. Scrambled eggs and toast for breakfast?" asks Albert.

"You are a godsend," says Paul.

"I'm in," says Bolton. "I need to do some shopping this morning and will replace what we eat."

"Nonsense," says Albert. "Consider this my treat. We've all put some cash into the shopping can. Take money from there. If you can haul a few bags of groceries, I'd like to start a list."

"I need a couple of things too," says Deena as her mobile phone rings. "Hello," she says and moves into the living room.

"I can help you shop," says Paul, who is setting the table with coffee mugs, dishes, and cutlery.

"Sounds like a plan," says Bolton who is putting bread in the toaster.

Deena comes back into the room. "That was Reggie," she says. He sprained his ankle shooting hoops last night with friends after the move. He was supposed to help me build a deck this morning..."

"Did he go to the hospital?" Albert asks as he scrambles eggs in a frying pan.

"He has ice and a tensor bandage on it and has it elevated. But it looks like he's off his feet for a couple of days. I can carry supplies, but I'm going to have to see if one of the other fellows who helps on occasion is available."

"You know," Albert says, "I did a fair bit of renovation before my diagnosis. As I told you, I'm pretty good with a hammer, screw driver, and saw. I can even plaster and paint. Paul and Bolton are going shopping. I've got nothing on my agenda today, so if you want a hand..."

"You sure?" asks Deena. "With Reggie, I carry stuff in, set it up, and supervise as he does most of the finesse work. My Parkinson's has me too shaky... I mean I can do some..."

"Say no more," says Albert scooping eggs on to plates. "Let's call it a trial. You haul stuff in--strength is not my greatest attribute--set it up and supervise, and I'll cut, hammer, and screw. If it works out, you have a new employee. If not, you are free to fire me."

"I pay just over minimum wage."

"Oh hell, today's trial is on the house. See if you like what I can do before we talk money."

"After breakfast then? We have some supplies to buy, and then a deck to build."

"I'm all yours."

Everybody sits at the table, with plates heaped full of scrambled eggs in front of them and a plate stacked with unbuttered toast in the middle of the table.

"Looks great," says Bolton. "But if there are no objections, I'm adding butter and bacon to the grocery list!"

After breakfast, Deena and Albert head out in Deena's van to buy wood and other supplies so they can work on the deck.

Paul walks with Bolton who scoots along in his wheelchair to the local No Frills grocery store. There they buy various food items and cleaning supplies, and then head home. With his cane, Paul can only lug two shopping bags. Bolton puts four bags on his lap.

When they get home, they put away the groceries, and then Paul says he needs to sit on the couch.

"Fatigue?" asks Bolton.

"Nah. Just general tiredness. Not going to pass out. Just need to sit."

"I'll get my laptop and, if you want, we can look at TV series to download and find some stuff to watch this evening."

"Sounds like a plan," Paul says as he puts his head back and shuts his eyes.

Bolton returns with his laptop and wheels in across from Paul. "It occurs to me that I'm probably up to date with downloads. There's a lot of stuff that I haven't watched yet, just sitting on my laptop. What's your fancy? Comedy? Drama? Police procedurals? Mind you, if you say period pieces, I will have to download some new programs."

"I like a good cop show."

"I've got several British cop shows that get excellent reviews."

"A British cop show this evening sounds like a plan," says Paul. His mobile phone beeps. "Ah, incoming email. If you don't mind, I should check this."

"Not a problem," says Bolton. "I've got some job research to do."

Bolton types away on his laptop while Paul taps on his phone keyboard and squints at his screen. "Damn it all," he says.

"Everything okay?" asks Bolton, looking up from his laptop.

"On my website, I say that I am taking time off from motivational speaking, or words to that effect. But I just received an email from a previous client, Nadir Knight in human resources at Canada One Bank. He asked me if I'd like to motivate some young entrepreneurs, clients of the bank, at a conference that Canada One is hosting…" Paul looks down at his phone. "…in about six months." Paul pauses and sighs deeply. "You have to understand, I used to live for stuff like this."

"As did I for running."

"Exactly. You understand. It's why I haven't taken down my website, and haven't called old clients to let them know I'm no longer in the speaking business. Now I have to tell Nadir I can't take on the engagement. I hate turning down work… I'll give it a day, and then email him."

"That sucks."

"As I'm sure not being able to run does."

"True that."

"Out of curiosity, and tell me to back off if I'm out of line, have you given up totally on athleticism?"

Bolton taps the wheels on his wheelchair in reply.

"That's a given. But what about para-events, the Paralympics even?"

Bolton shrugs, exhales, and purses his lips. "Not something I've thought about. I mean, I had to recover from the accident just to get into the chair, and then there was parting with my girlfriend, and then finding a place to live… I'm a business graduate from the University of Toronto. I had a job in website design and social media promotion with a company that supported my running by giving me time off to train and compete.

I guess now I'm just focused on finding a job, any job, so I can pay my rent and contribute more to our grocery fund."

"Again, if I'm out of line…"

"Talk away. I don't mind."

"You said you didn't get an insurance settlement because you caused the accident, but aren't you on some kind of disability salary?"

"No insurance. And no disability. The company I worked for let me go. And I don't blame them, under the circumstances. You don't get a disability salary if you're not employed."

Paul puts down his phone and leans forward. "So now it's find a job, or…?"

"Exactly."

"But while you're looking for work, couldn't you try to make, I don't know, a para-sprinting team? I mean you obviously love to race."

"Tell you what," says Bolton. "I'll make you a deal. You email Nadir and tell him you'll take the speaking gig, and I'll look into trying out for the Toronto wheelchair racing team."

Paul laughs. "Damn, man. You're motivating me when I was trying to motivate you." He pauses and looks at his phone. "Let me make sure I have this right. I accept the speaking gig and you try out for the Toronto wheelchair racing team?"

"That about sums it up."

"But what if you don't make the team?"

"Then I'll have time to come to your speaking event!"

"But the talk is for entrepreneurs… Wait a second. See that light bulb above my head?"

Bolton looks up with a smile. "Let's say that I see it. Why is it on?"

"You create websites and know social media. You shouldn't be looking for a job. You should be using what you know to sell your skills. You can make your own work, in an entrepreneurial manner, and then come to the talk. With that in mind, here's the deal, if interested. I accept the speaking gig. You try out for the racing team and start a website design and social media marketing business."

"That's quite the light bulb," says Bolton. "You said you weren't going to reply to Nadir for a day?"

"Correct."

"Okay, let me look into a few things and I'll get back to you with how you should reply based on some research I need to do."

Paul holds out his hand to air-shake with Bolton. "You're on. Now if you don't mind, I'm going to my room to set up my painting paraphernalia. I feel a picture coming on. Although I may pass out first."

"And I have some research to do, and some calls to make. One in particular."

*   *   *

Deena and Albert drive to Home Hardware where Albert buys enough pressure-treated boards to build an elevated nine by twelve first floor deck with a bench and three steps down to the backyard lawn. "This is going to be a good place for you to start. Plain deck, other than the bench, with a modest foundation, no railing, and three steps. Mostly cutting and hammering and staining when it's all done."

"I've never built a deck before," says Albert. "But I've done a lot of cutting and hammering, so you tell me what and where to cut, place, and hammer, and all should work out fine."

"If it does, and you enjoy the work, I can quote on larger jobs that we, along with my son, can handle."

As they are driving away from Home Hardware, Albert says, "I don't mean to pry, but your son looks young."

"Turned sixteen not all that long ago."

"Won't he be going back to school come the fall?"

"He says he's going to be a dropout, like his old man. He believes if construction is his future, then why wait. I'm trying to encourage him to finish high school and get his B.A. or a college diploma, but he says that won't help him cut, hammer, screw, drywall, paint, or stain."

"Like mother, like son, eh? When did you quit school and start doing renovation and repair work?"

"I always had summer construction jobs, so when I left school, going out on my own was a kind of natural thing to do."

"And what grade did you complete? Not judging in any way. Just curious."

"Greek Literature PhD student."

"What?"

"Yep. I was working on my PhD and I thought, 'What the heck am I doing?' I mean, I enjoy the classics, but I've got nothing to contribute to anybody's understanding of them. It took me a while to realize that I was drowning in a fake thirst for obscure knowledge when I could feel more fulfilled hammering a nail or turning a screw to fix a broken-down railing or some such."

Albert laughs. "Like me taking a temperature so I can help fix a fever or some such."

"You fix people and I fix things," Deena says as she pulls her van into a driveway. "I'll unload the wood while you unload the tool box, drill, and rake for leveling the ground. Then we'll get started."

When they get to the back yard, they see Harold Reckon, the contractor who hired Deena for the deck job, talking to the Sarbanes, the home owners. Harold is a tall, slender man who is almost fifty, although he looks younger. His hair is long and tangled, but clean with a hint of grey at his temples. His face is tanned, slim, and mostly wrinkle-free. "Here are my men, or persons, I should say," Harold exclaims. "Right on time."

Deena introduces Albert to Harold who then introduces them both to the Sarbanes. "The job is pretty straight forward," Harold says. "How long do you estimate it will take you to complete it?"

"Should be done in three days," says Deena putting down a pile of deck planks. "Maybe a fourth day for the final coat of stain."

"Is there more of that in the van?" asks Harold. "If so, let me help you with it."

"Put down the tools and take the lay of the land," Deena says to Albert as she and Harold walk to the van.

On the way, Harold says, "No son today?"

"Ankle injury."

"Albert is not one of your regulars."

"First time with me," Deena says. "A great guy."

"A bit, you know, swishy. No?"

Deena opens the van's back doors, pulls out as much wood as she can, and piles it in Harold's outstretched arms, almost knocking him over. "And you're a little macho. No? How about we judge by the work?"

"Ah, you know me. How long did it take me to get used to you, being a woman who does renovations?"

Deena pulls the last of the wood out of the van. "Do you want to carry this too? That would be the macho thing to do."

"I know you can handle it, and I'm sure your man will do well on the job or he wouldn't be working with you."

"We'll do just fine," says Deena as she starts to walk toward the backyard, Harold trailing after her lugging several long deck planks. When she gets to the back, she sees Albert hard at work, raking the earth level where the deck is going to be built. "We'll do just fine."

Chapter Three

Paul Amil is dreaming that he is doing... only he doesn't know what he is doing. It seems to involve climbing, but from where to where he hasn't a clue. His limbs are straining as he climbs, until he wakes up muddled, confused, and reaching for something that is not there.

*   *   *

The roommates have been eating takeout or sandwiches for dinner for several days as they settle in and adjust to their new living together routines. For their first official stay-at-home-and-cook evening together, Bolton offers to make pasta. "Sauce from a jar, though. I imagine we can experiment more with gourmet cooking later when we have the time and energy to cook creatively," he laughs.

"At some point, you'll get to taste my honey-garlic chicken!" says Albert.

"We bought some romaine lettuce. I can whip up a Caesar salad to go with the pasta," Paul says. "I make a mean dressing, with or without bacon. I don't think there are any vegetarians in the room. If so, speak now or forever hold your peace."

"I'm in for bacon on my Caesar," says Deena. Albert and Bolton murmur their agreement.

"We have butter pecan ice cream for dessert, for those interested," says Bolton as he fills a pot with water for the pasta.

"Then we've got a complete meal: carbs, protein, vegetables, and sugar," says Paul. "Not the Wahl's Protocol Diet that some folks with MS are on. But healthy enough."

"Think I've heard of that diet," muses Albert. "Studies are going on around it."

"Written by a doctor with MS. Took her from wheelchair to bike riding. She still has MS, but is much better. Others I know who have tried it haven't had miracle results, but it hasn't killed anybody," Paul replies while busy at the counter.

Chronic

Deena and Albert set the table as Paul and Bolton cook. "The only thing we don't have is beer or wine," says Albert. "But just so you folks know, I don't drink alcohol. I used to, but ever since the diagnosis..." His voice trails off.

"I'm with you," says Paul as he tosses the salad. "I'm dizzy enough sober."

"And I'm shaky enough without booze," adds Deena.

"And I've crashed enough cars with it, so I'm happy to pass," adds Bolton with a wry tone, and then a half-hearted laugh. "I mean if you can't joke about it..."

"...it wins," says Paul completing Bolton's thought. "And there will be no diseases, sicknesses, or maladies winning in this house."

"Amen to that," says Deena.

"Agreed!" Albert laughs.

Over dinner, as people are sprinkling parmesan cheese on their pasta and filling their glasses with ginger ale or water, Paul suggests that they get to know each other more formally. "We take turns talking about ourselves, our issues, what we do or no longer do, for five minutes or so each."

Everybody agrees, so Paul asks, "Any volunteers to go first?"

Albert swallows a forkful of pasta. "No time like the present," he says, clearing his throat.

"All right, Albert, the floor is yours," says Paul to laughter around the table.

"As you know, I was a nurse and I now have, or am in remission from, lung cancer. When, or if, it returns, nobody knows... And by the way, keep on eating while I talk." To demonstrate his point, Albert takes another forkful of pasta. Everybody digs into their pasta.

"Good point," says Paul as he reaches for the Caesar salad.

"I'm being watched closely to see if the cancer becomes active again and I'm on maintenance chemotherapy to help thwart its return. I loved nursing, or helping to fix people as I called it, but I've had to go on disability leave. My strength and stamina aren't what they used to be. I have some disability money coming in, and if I do another job with Deena, I'm going to insist on at least minimum wage!"

"You're on," Deena agrees.

Albert takes another mouthful of pasta and chews it down. "Oh, and there was my relationship with Leon. We had just moved in together when I was diagnosed. I told him he should find somebody healthy. He agreed, at my prodding. He did what I probably would have done had the shoe been on the other foot."

Albert reaches for the salad. "A final thought. Pet peeve. People who say, 'You look good' as if that means I am fine. I feel like crap, even in remission. I have cancer. The maintenance chemo takes it out of me. Looking good has nothing to do with what's going on in my body. And that's about it."

"People saying, 'You look good' drives me crazy too. It feels dismissive," Paul chimes in. "Ask me how I'm doing, don't tell me how I look, as if you are denying how I am."

"So true," agrees Deena.

"Anyway, thanks, Albert," says Paul. "Next?"

"Well, since my new workmate went first, I should go next," says Deena. She takes a sip of soda. "First off, I must say that Albert knows his way around a saw and hammer and nails. The deck we worked on is in place and as sturdy as it should be. We go back tomorrow to varnish it, and it's job done."

Deena clears her throat. "Where to officially begin?" she asks rhetorically. "As you know, I have Parkinson's and my hands and arms often shake, along with a couple of other issues. My son, Reggie, whom you met the day we moved in, has been working with me on renovation work. He injured his ankle so Albert is filling in. Admirably, I must say. When my son comes back to work, I hope the three of us can bid on larger jobs, and finish the smaller ones faster."

Albert lifts his glass of water in Deena's direction in a toast.

"Oh, and I told Albert so I should tell all of you, for my summer jobs, I worked in construction and renovation. I was a PhD student in Greek literature but quit to start my own renovation business. Reggie is taking after me, only quitting school years earlier. He hasn't even finished high school! We'll see how that goes."

Chronic

Deena sips at her ginger ale. "As for my Parkinson's, I was on Carbidopa-levodopa, the most effective Parkinson's medication going. However, I experienced nausea. Instead of shaking violently, I'd shake less violently, feel dizzy, and puke. Pick your poison. In addition, after several years, as my disease progressed, the benefits from Carbidopa-levodopa became less effective but the side effects remained, which is why I'm on nothing but fate now."

Deena takes another sip. "Let's see," she continues. "My ex emotionally left me around the time I lost interest in sex. I just could not flail about, panting sensually any longer. But I don't blame him. He deserves a life. At least we got a son out of our relationship. Reggie is living with Gilbert and Gilbert and I are mostly civil, if not a bit frosty, towards each other. He can be a bit of a jerk at times, although I may be biased."

Everybody laughs and Deena pauses to munch on some Caesar salad. "This is incredible dressing, Paul. Garlicky and creamy too." She takes another bite, chews, and swallows. "Medication is strange. I mean you break your arm, the doctors mend it and give you some pain killers. In six weeks or so, you're playing catch. With cancer, I presume you need the chemo or you die. You put up with the side effects."

"It's why I shave my head, what was left of my hair," says Albert with a chuckle. "But chemo isn't always a cure."

"As with Parkinson's, the meds are a crapshoot. The meds help some people, but not everybody. And the side effects can be as bad as the disease for some of us."

"As with MS," Paul says wryly.

"Similar, then," says Deena as she rolls the last forkful of pasta on her plate. "As for my pet peeve, it's people who imply that you are faking it. Like I'm faking my shaking. I want to say to them, 'I am faking being well so that I can get on with life as best I can." She sighs. "And that's about it from me."

"Faking being well. I never thought of it that way, but it is so what we do," says Paul. "If we went through life manifesting how we were feeling all the time, I suspect we'd never get out of bed."

"So true," says Bolton. "Like I want to use my arms to wheel through my day? But it's what I have to do if I want a life."

"Do you want to keep on talking, Bolton?" says Paul. "Not that I'm saving the best for last."

Bolton takes a drink of water. His plate is cleared of pasta and salad. "Okay, I'll go," he says. "First off, I want to thank you for letting me become your roommate."

"Worked out all 'round," says Albert.

Bolton toasts him with his water glass. "As I've mentioned, I was trying out for the Canadian Olympic sprint team and lost the last race of the indoor season. I drank, did coke, and smashed up my car. I'm in a wheelchair, but you should see the light post I took out..." He pauses. There is mild laughter, and he continues. "At least I can say I did not kill or injure anybody, other than myself. I no longer drink or do drugs, not just because I can't afford to drink or snort. Being in this chair is bad enough. I'm determined to ride it sober."

Bolton sips his water. "In other news, Paul has issued a challenge. I'll let him talk about what I challenged him to do, but he suggested I try out for a wheelchair sprint team. Tryouts are coming up next week. And instead of looking for a job, he wondered if I might be able to sell my website design and social media marketing services. I have my first client, non-paid. I'll be creating and promoting a website for Santali, whom you met on moving day. Santali and I are no longer together because I told her she had to get on with her life. But we're still friends."

Bolton sighs, takes another sip, and continues. "Anyhow, she makes dripless, scented candles that we'll try to sell online. I'm building a website for her. When that is done, I'll use social media to promote it. If that works, if she sells some candles, she becomes the first client success story that I'll put on my website, which I have to build." Bolton pushes his chair back from the table and stretches his arms up working out a kink in his back.

"You okay?" asks Paul.

"Just a kink. Happens a fair bit when your body's motion is limited. But I work them out," he says. "As for my pet peeve, people know what happened to me and still ask, 'When are you getting out of the chair?' One, never. And two, never is not something I want to think about. But thanks for asking. And with that... Paul."

Chronic

Paul pushes his empty pasta plate toward the middle of the table. "Bolton heard me moaning about a previous client asking me to speak at a conference. When I thought I was motivating Bolton to try out for the wheelchair racing team, he motivated me to accept the speaking job. I've called Nadir and accepted the gig."

"Cool," says Deena as Paul fills his glass with ginger ale from the bottle on the table.

"Not sure about that," says Paul, "in large part because of the progression of my MS. I have relapsing-remitting multiple sclerosis or RRMS, the most common type of the disease. Sometimes I have tingles, pain, or eye issues that last for weeks or a month or two, and then go, and I'll be fine for a month or two, other than the fatigue, which can hit at any time. In theory, the various hits don't keep me from doing my work. But the fatigue does. Loved working as a motivational speaker and writer…"

Paul picks up his glass of ginger ale but does not drink. "The fatigue literally knocks me out for thirty minutes or more. I come to feeling as groggy as when I passed out. Hence the fear of public speaking, or passing out on stage. Also, now my knees are wonky and I'm kind of dizzy, which is why I walk with a cane. But I can still paint, something that was a fun hobby for me. I've set up my easel and paint in my room, and hope to get at it sooner rather than later… At least I don't have Primary Progressive MS, the worst kind, like Martha's husband had. Something to be thankful for, I suppose. Could be worse. Feels like a perverse mantra."

Paul inhales deeply. "As for meds, when I was first diagnosed with MS, there were only a few meds on the market, with not very pleasant potential side effects. I tried several. Aubagio didn't seem to do anything, other than make me feel nauseous and give me diarrhea. Then Gilenya. Did it do anything? I don't know."

"What are they supposed to do?" asks Bolton.

"They are supposed to provide some control over the inflammation that injures nerves, reduce the frequency and severity of relapses, and ease the impact of MS symptoms."

Paul swirls the ginger ale in his glass. "But when I asked my neurologist, 'To what extent do they reduce the frequency of relapses?' She said one couldn't be sure. My disease progressed but my neurologist says it might have progressed faster without the drugs. Nobody knows for sure. Anyway, I decided to go med-free about three years ago."

Paul takes a deep breath. "There are more meds on the market now but I don't take anything. One med seems to work for one person but not for another person. Some people get side effects with no benefits. Some get benefits with no side effects. It's a bizarre world. I did try medical marijuana for three months about a year ago. Had symptoms and spent more time at Tim Hortons eating donuts." Paul grins at the memory as everybody laughs.

Albert says, "I take CBD oil before I go to bed. It's made from marijuana but with THC, the element that gets you high, removed. It seems to relax me and helps me sleep, but it sure as hell isn't going to cure me."

"Maybe I should try it," says Deena. "From what I've heard, it can't hurt. And if it helps…"

"Happy to let you try mine," says Albert.

"And maybe I should try the Wahl's Protocol diet," says Paul. "It seems to have helped some people with MS, but not everybody. It hasn't hurt anybody, unless you count the increased cost of food and the complexity of making it."

Everybody laughs at this, and Paul continues. "I too have a pet peeve. People who imply that it's all in my head and say that I should meditate. I want to say, 'If I punch you and break your nose, can you meditate through that?' MS, and what we are all dealing with, is physical, not mental. I'm not saying meditating can't help you relax or that being positive can't help you feel better mentally. I am saying that neither is a cure for MS."

"Sadly, so true," agrees Deena.

"I guess I have a speaking engagement coming up in a few months," says Paul. "I think I'll go to bed now and one of you can wake me the day I'm supposed to speak. Maybe I'll be so rested I won't pass out while talking."

Paul lifts his glass of ginger ale and takes a long drink.

"It's all so bizarre," adds Albert. "Cancer. You get treatment and you go into remission, or you don't. Neither outcome has anything to do with your attitude or with you as a person. Sometimes, you get treatment and you die."

"Or there is a disease-modifying drug that may, or may not, help alleviate symptoms, but it won't cure you," says Deena. "Overall, it's a crapshoot. Kind of like life."

"That's what people who aren't sick don't get. We got hit by the bus. They could get hit tomorrow," Paul says.

"So true," sighs Albert. "And why is it that people who have no maladies assume that people with disabilities or diseases must be miserable?"

"I was initially," says Paul.

"As was I," says Bolton.

"Me too. Big time," adds Albert. "But you need time to adjust and work through it."

"I get the feeling that we've all adjusted. I'm sure we have our moments, but we've learned how to live with whatever plagues us," says Deena.

"What choice do we have?" asks Albert.

"I guess we can choose to not adjust," Bolton states matter-of-factly. "Not my choice, but it's an option."

"People who are well can be even more miserable than we are!" Paul points out, to which his roommates nod in agreement.

"And with all that in mind, who wants butter pecan ice cream for dessert?" asks Bolton.

"Definitely not on the Wahl's diet," says Paul. "But neither am I, yet, so I'll take a healthy scoop.

"I'm with you," says Deena.

"Count me in," adds Albert.

"Four bowls of pecan ice cream coming up," says Bolton as he wheels away from the table and heads towards the fridge.

* * *

After dinner, the roommates sit in the living room, somewhat ill at ease and at loose ends. Bolton has his laptop in his lap, but it is not open. Albert is on the couch holding a book but is not reading. Paul is also on the couch, his head back and eyes closed. Deena is slouched in a chair doing nothing.

"I think," Paul says as he opens his eyes, "we are thinking that we are somehow supposed to amuse each other." His three roommates laugh nervously. "So here is what I propose. After dinner, which is fun to eat together, we go our separate ways unless we have something specific to do together. What do you usually do in the evening, Bolton?"

"I normally watch TV shows on my laptop with my headphones plugged in, so if folks wanted to watch something else on TV, I'm okay with that."

"Or you can connect your laptop to the TV and we can watch British cop shows," says Paul. "What about you, Albert?"

"Evenings are tough. Mostly I read or do some writing. Not a big TV watcher, but not opposed to it. If you folks are out here watching something, I'm happy to read or write in the bedroom if I'm not interested in watching."

"Since I'm locked in my chair until I go to bed, it doesn't matter where I am," Bolton shrugs.

"Deena?"

"Albert's right. The evenings are the toughest. If I have work to do, I may ponder it. I've watched a lot of crap TV, so British shows would be a nice change of pace. What about you, Paul?"

"Mostly, I sit with my eyes closed until it's time to go to bed. I have set up my easel in the bedroom and am trying to get back into painting. But I like a good detective mystery, so I'd be happy to watch what Bolton has downloaded. But we're not responsible for amusing each other. Having said that, if folks aren't into anything yet..."

"I think Paul is about to amuse us," says Deena.

"Only if you want. You are free to leave the room at any time, or to turn on the TV, or plop on your headphones, and tell me to piss off."

"I'm in," says Albert.

"Me too," says Deena.

"Shoot," says Bolton. "The videos on my computer aren't going anywhere."

"It's kind of silly, but I'm curious. Has anybody looked up celebrities or other famous people who are dealing with what they are dealing with? I suspect we are all in good company."

"Me first!" says Deena excitedly. "I've got a great shared-with-the-rich-and-famous illness." Everybody laughs.

"Do tell," says Albert.

"Okay, the most famous person with Parkinson's is Michael J. Fox. He's using his celebrity status to help others with the disease. Check out his website, The Micheal J. Fox Foundation for Parkinson's Research. The Foundation is dedicated to finding a cure for Parkinson's, not that it will happen in my lifetime, and to develop improved therapies for those living with Parkinson's."

"It's unfortunate that he has the disease, but sounds like he is using his energy in a positive manner to fight it," says Albert.

"That he is."

"Are there others?" asks Paul.

"Almost an endless list. Muhammad Ali had Parkinson's, as did George H.W. Bush and the preacher Billy Graham. Alan Alda of *M.A.S.H.* fame has it, as does the British comedian Billy Connolly and the singers Neil Diamond, Ozzy Osbourne, and Linda Rondstadt. So I feel like I'm in good company. What about you, Paul?"

"I'm glad this isn't a contest! But some people you may have heard of have MS. Selma Blair, the actress, has it"

"From *Cruel Intentions*?" asks Bolton.

"The one and only. Also, the actress Jamie-Lynn Sigler, the daughter Meadow in *The Sopranos*, has it."

"I was going to download that series. Worth it?" asks Bolton.

"I'd watch it again," says Paul.

"I'm in," says Deena.

"I missed it the first time around," adds Albert.

"I'll look for it then."

"The comedian Richard Pryor had it and, because you're a reader Albert, I suspect you'd know that the author, Joan Didion, had MS."

"She won a National Book Award for her memoir *The Year of Magical Thinking*. She was a Pulitzer Prize finalist and, if I recall correctly, she received a National Medal of Honor from President Obama."

"Finally, the singer Drake doesn't have it, but his producer Noah Shebib does. Drake has sung about him a couple of times, although I suspect most people miss the references to Noah and his disease in the songs. They're subtle. What about you, Albert?"

"If I can include all cancers, not just lung cancer, we have an interesting list."

"Let me check the rules..." Paul pretends to be flipping through pages of a booklet. "Yes, you may."

"Thank you, my good man," Albert says with a bow and a laugh. "I suspect most of you didn't know that Jane Fonda had lip cancer."

"Did not know that," says Deena.

"If you watched *Seinfeld* and *VEEP*, you might know that Julia Louis-Dreyfus was diagnosed with breast cancer. She's doing okay, as far as I know. Ben Stiller..."

"From *Tropic Thunder*, *Zoolander*, and *Night at the Museum*?" asks Bolton.

"That would be him. He survived prostate cancer. An older actress, Melanie Griffith, had skin cancer some time ago. Not sure how she is doing now. Academy Award-winning actor, Dustin Hoffman, has been treated for an unspecified form of cancer. Too shy to say, I suppose. Oh, and talk-show host Larry King... drum roll please... had my cancer, lung cancer. Finally, a man who died from his cancer, the late singer David Bowie. He was diagnosed with liver cancer."

"Loved his music," Paul says. "Had him on vinyl, cassette tape, and CD."

"If you want, I can download his music and put it on your laptop," says Bolton.

"You mean I don't have to subscribe to Spotify to hear him?"

"Not if you don't want to."

"Sounds cool," Paul laughs. "Now how about famous people in wheelchairs?"

"I think I've got the most intelligent sick person ever. The late, great Stephen Hawking. His ALS put him in a wheelchair, took away his voice and who knows what else. But he just kept on keeping on. The late Christopher Reeve, the man known for playing the unbreakable Superman, broke his neck during an equestrian competition. That put him in a wheelchair. But my favourite person in a wheelchair was… Ironside."

"Hey," says Paul, "he was a TV character played by, who…?

"Raymond Burr!" answers Deena. "He was able-bodied when he played Ironside.

"Ironically, later in life he became ill and needed to use a wheelchair," says Bolton. "I'm working my way through eight seasons, one hundred and ninety-five episodes of the show."

"There should be more people in wheelchairs, with disabilities, illnesses, and diseases on TV and in movies and books," says Albert. "Instead, it's like society hides us away, in houses or hospitals."

"So how do we break free?" asks Bolton. "I'm not saying how do we become famous. Most of the folks we've talked about achieved their celebrity status before their illness, disease, or malady overtook them. I'm saying how do we who are sick exist outside of the shadows?"

"We exist by doing," says Paul. "I know that can be difficult for each of us for different reasons, but that is how we exist. By doing what we can do, to the best of our abilities."

"Well, Deena and Albert are doing. And you've challenged me to do, and I've challenged you to do. I guess we know, difficult as it can be, what we have to do if we want to exist outside the shadows. We know what we have to freaking do!"

*　　*　　*

A month passes. The roommates settle into a routine. Paul does a little painting, mostly small images that he is not really satisfied with. He also works on several articles for clients. Deena and Albert take on several more renovation jobs. When his ankle heals, Reggie works with them, although he takes some time off to go camping with his buddies. Bolton works on Santali's candle website, trying to get its look and feel just right. He starts, albeit slowly, to put his website together and, in response to his wheelchair racing inquiry, he gets a call from the coach of the Toronto wheelchair racing team inviting him to the racing team try outs.

*   *   *

Paul has an appoint with Dr. Jan Wong, his Saint Mike's MS Clinic neurologist. As usual, the appointment is several weeks after he's had an MRI to check on how his MS lesions are progressing.

"How are you doing today?" says Dr. Wong, a tall, thin Asian woman with straight black hair cascading over her shoulders.

"You're the doctor. You tell me," Paul says with a laugh.

Dr. Wong smiles. "Let's start with your MRI results."

"Let me guess. I have MS."

Dr. Wong ignores his comment and points to various spots on his MRI results, displayed on the computer screen on her desk. "Several of your lesions have diminished in size, several have grown. Others are static. And you only have one new one, but it's relatively small."

"Dr. Wong, I don't mean to interrupt you, but I have to tell you something, "Paul says. His neurologist nods. "This is my last visit."

"Why is that?" asks Dr. Wong in a professional tone.

"I've been coming here for over a decade. We tried one medication to help me and I had a horrible reaction. We tried another one and maybe it increased the time between hits and their severity. We don't really know, do we?"

"It can be difficult to tell. But you did well for several years," says Dr. Wong as she flips through Paul's file.

"If I move from RRMS to secondary progressive, I will get fewer hits but they won't go away, correct?"

"Yes, but you are not there yet."

"Dr. Wong, you have a lovely bedside manner, and my sympathy."

"Sympathy?"

"You are unable to tell anyone with MS that they are getting better or will be cured. I'm off meds because we don't know that they worked. We do know that they caused other issues. I've been thinking about trying the Wahl's Protocol diet."

"It won't hurt, but it's not a proven solution. It is undergoing tests as we speak."

Paul holds up his hand. "Nothing is proven. And Wahl's will hurt me, forcing me to give up ice cream, which isn't on the diet."

Dr. Wong laughs and waits for him to continue.

"Can you give me one medically solid reason for having annual MRIs and then coming to see you?"

Dr. Wong hesitates. "We get to see how you are doing. How you are progressing," she says.

"I'm doing, excuse my language, shitty. I am regressing. I have MS. It's not going away. I'm just going to get on with my life until I no longer can."

Dr. Wong looks at Paul with a degree of intensity. "May that day be far, far away."

Paul uses his cane to help himself get up and holds out a hand. "Thank you for everything, Dr. Wong."

Dr. Wong air-shakes his hand and gives him a post-pandemic hug by embracing herself. "All the best to you. And if you ever change your mind, please call the clinic and make an appointment to see me."

"If I read about a cure for MS, calling you is the first thing I'll do."

Chapter Four

Paul is dreaming that he is playing basketball. As he dribbles down the floor, his opponents start throwing basketballs at him, as if they are playing dodge ball. Paul can't dodge the balls and gets hit repeatedly. He is still able to step back and sink a three-pointer, nothing but net, and raises his arms in celebration as a ball hits him in the face. Paul wakes in a sweat and grasps his nose, thinking that it might be bleeding.

*   *   *

That morning over a breakfast of Shreddies and orange juice, Paul is rubbing his eyes.

"Problem?" asks Deena as she fills her bowl with Corn Flakes.

"My optic neuritis is flaring up. Again. It's always different. Today I can look at you and make your head disappear with a black spot that's in my right eye." Paul laughs. "But more than enough about sickness and symptoms. Who is doing what today?" he asks his roommates who are sitting around the table enjoying their breakfasts.

"Albert and I, if you are up to another day another dollar, Albert, are starting a new paint job, for Harold," Deena says. "At the end of the day, we have to go see a house that needs its basement refinished. Mostly drywall, taping, and painting. Harold wants me to quote on the job."

"I'm up to it. I thought Reggie would replace me when he came back from his ankle injury, then his camping trip, but the three of us seem to work well together."

"If we land the basement reno and can get multiple jobs on the go, there will be more than enough work for all of us." Deena scoops up a mouthful of cereal.

"I'll be making Santali's website an e-commerce site so she can sell her candles online. Then I have to start the social media promotion and optimize it for search engines so that it shows up when people search for candles, dripless candles, and other related terms."

"Search engines? Other than Google?" asks Albert.

"Google is the largest search engine by far, but there is Microsoft's Bing and several others. You want to be in all of them."

"Hey," says Deena, "what would it cost me to get a site on the web? If I could bring in business without going through Harold, I'd make more money per job."

"I need a couple of clients for my website, which I have started to build, so I'd create a three pager--home page about your company, a page of pictures and testimonials for work you've done, and a contact page--all for a testimonial to my amazing ability that I could put on my site with a link to yours. All you'd have to do is pay for the domain name and a hosting fee, maybe two hundred dollars in total for year one."

"A deal like that, you're on. I have pictures of jobs that I've completed and should be able to dig up a few testimonials."

"Have you got pictures of the work you did at my old place? If so, I'm your first testimonial," says Paul. "You write it. I'll sign it. If you don't have pictures, Quelina will let you take some shots."

"You're on," says Deena.

"What about you, Paul?" asks Albert.

"I have to email Nadir a few questions. Nail down the exact date and time of the speaking gig. He's been sorting that out. Find out exactly how long he needs me to talk and who the primary audience is. And then I am either painting, I have a vague idea for a larger painting percolating, or going to Another Story Bookstore to find a Wahl's Protocol book. Seriously thinking of trying a dietary change."

Deena gives Paul the thumbs up. "If you do, let me know. I'll think about trying it too."

"You are what you eat," says Albert. "I'd look at the book and think it over."

"I know I should say something inclusive here," says Bolton. He takes a mouthful of Shreddies. "But we just bought so much stuff that I'm sure is not on the Wahl's diet."

"I wouldn't ask any of you to go on the diet with me. I'm not even sure I'm going on it. If I do, it will be after I've finished my share of the licorice we just bought and a couple of other delicacies we have that I suspect are not on the diet."

Everybody laughs and Deena picks up her dishes and gets up. "Shall we start the day?" she asks Albert.

"I'm with you," Albert replies, pushing away from the table and putting his dishes in the dishwasher after Deena.

"Remind me to tell you about some tax stuff you need to know now that you are a freelance renovator, that is if you are going to report what I pay you," says Deena.

"Always honest come tax time," says Albert. "Paranoid about being audited."

"Render unto Caesar. A healthy attitude, I'd say."

"But not a penny more than you owe," Paul chirps with a laugh as he loads his dishes in the dishwasher. "Let the day begin!"

Bolton sits at the table for a while and says to the room that has emptied, "Wheelchair racing. I forgot to tell them that I will be trying out for the Toronto team in a couple of weeks." He shrugs, picks up his dish, spoon, and glass, wheels over to the dishwasher and loads them in. He rolls into the living room and opens his laptop to see if Santali has sent him the final pictures of some new candles she wants featured on her website. She has. "I guess the day has truly begun." He then closes his laptop and stares at the wall for a moment before he begins to tear up. He inhales deeply and wipes at his eyes with a sleeve. "Purpose. I never thought I'd ever feel that again."

A few minutes later, he reopens the laptop and starts to work.

*   *   *

At dinner, Bolton remembers to tell his roommates that he's been invited to try out for the wheelchair racing team. "I'm going to be lifting weights and racing around High Park for the next couple of weeks. I'm at a disadvantage because I have to train using my chair, not a racing chair, but my chair is heavier than a racing chair, so it will be good for my arms. And I'll get a racing chair loaner for the tryout."

"Lemon. Lemonade," says Paul.

"The alternative was to turn down the invite," says Bolton.

"Damn, I could have backed out of my talk," moans Paul.

"Not on my watch!" says Bolton with a grin.

After dinner, as the roommates are sitting around the living room drinking tea, there's a knock on the door to the flat. Albert gets up to answer it. "Hey Martha," his friends hear him say. "Come on in."

Martha pokes her head into the flat. "It's been just over a month since you folks moved in. You've told me, informally when we've bumped into each other, that all is going well. I'm just checking to make sure you have adapted to living here and to see if there is anything you need."

"All is fine," says Paul.

"Having the flat furnished was a godsend," says Bolton.

"I think we have everything we need," adds Deena.

"And still too much cutlery!" quips Albert.

"Do you want to come in for tea?" asks Paul. "I can put the kettle back on."

"Thank you, but I don't want to intrude. Just thought I should do a quick check on my tenants."

The front door to the house opens. Martha and Albert hear Genevieve coming in.

Looking over Martha's shoulder, Albert calls, "Come on in, Genevieve. Just a little chit-chat going on."

"Hi honey," says Martha. "How was the study group?"

Genevieve sighs as they enter the flat. "The group is struggling to wrap its collective head around the *Iliad* and the *Odyssey*. But I won't bore everybody with that."

"Oh my," says Albert, "are you a classic Greek literature major?"

"English. This is an elective that I thought would be, I don't know, not necessarily easy, but fun in a different way."

"Shall I tell them or do you want to keep a wrap on it?" Paul asks Deena.

"Go ahead," says Deena. "Spill my beans. Out me."

"What beans would that be?" asks Genevieve.

"Deena was a Greek literature PhD student, before life in construction," says Paul.

"Oh my," exclaims Martha. "PhD?"

"I dropped out to pursue honest labour."

"So, you've studied…?" asks Genevieve.

"Even taught the two poems."

"Would you… I mean if I texted you with the date and time of our study group's next meeting, do you think you could spare an evening?" asks Genevieve.

"Your mom has my mobile number. Text away! Wouldn't hurt to put my education to a modest use."

Everybody laughs.

"Do we need to set up a chalkboard?" asks Genevieve.

"Don't think there will be much more than a bit of chatting," says Deena.

"Thank you so much," Genevieve says with a smile.

Martha puts an arm around Genevieve's shoulder. "We have taken enough of your time tonight. If anything is ever amiss, just knock on our door." She and Genevieve head out as the roommates wish them goodnight.

"With that, I'm going to my room to paint, unless I pass out first," says Paul.

"I'll be refining Santali's website. The goal is to go live tomorrow," says Bolton. "Then I'll be racing in High Park."

"I'm going to my room to create a video blog," says Deena. "It's something I've been thinking about doing for a while. Just not sure if I want a renovation video blog or a life with Parkinson's one."

"A renovation one would look cool on your website," says Bolton.

"Couldn't you do both, as the spirit moves you?" asks Albert.

"I suppose I have time for both," says Deena. "I certainly have stuff to say about both."

"I'm hitting the sack," Albert says to Bolton. "Again, don't worry about lights or noise when you come in. I'll be in a CBD oil state of sleep."

"I still have to get a CBD hit off you," says Deena with a grin.

Chronic

The roommates say a final goodnight.

In his room, Paul puts down his cane, breaks out his paints, picks up a paintbrush, and looks at an extra large canvas that he has set up. He puts his brush down and pulls down the blankets on his bed. He then turns back to the canvas, picks up his brush, squirts some red, yellow, and blue on a palette, and blends the paints. He under-paints his background with blended strokes. He steps back and looks at his very preliminary work.

"There. Now I can go pass out."

* * *

The next day, Paul limps to the bookstore on the main drag and buys a copy of the Wahl's Protocol book. When he gets home, he sits in the living room and thumbs through it. Bolton comes in from the kitchen. "What are you reading?" he asks.

"Wahl's Protocol, which I am finding rather depressing. I wouldn't force this on anybody. It's not disgusting, but it means giving up one of the few joys I have in life. Great food, including my kind of dessert."

"No butter pecan ice cream?"

"There is Wahl's fudge. Walnuts, avocado, coconut milk, cocoa powder, topped with berries and cream from the coconut milk."

"Sounds sort of vaguely interesting," Bolton says with a smile.

"But you don't eat dairy products, eggs, or grains, including wheat, rice, and oatmeal. What will I eat for breakfast? And you don't have legumes like beans and lentils. It's not a disaster, but it would take a lot of work to do and to get used to. I'm not very motivated to change my way of eating right now, I confess. It's not like I eat, or we eat, poorly. I just don't eat Wahl's."

* * *

That evening, over a macaroni and cheese dinner prepared by Albert, Paul tosses out a question. "I'm just curious, what were folks like when first diagnosed, or in your case Bolton, when you first realized the wheelchair was your home for life?"

48

"Oh man," replies Bolton. "I was a mess. I wanted to do cocaine again, even though that was what put me in this chair. And I don't know how Santali put up with me, with my anger and depression. I was either yelling or crying, until the day I told her that I had to leave. It wasn't her fault, but I couldn't find myself while living with somebody who cared for me and about me. I had to learn how to care for and about myself."

He stabs at his macaroni and cheese. "I won't say that I'm there yet, but I feel like I'm moving in the right direction. Not that I'll never feel depressed about what I did to myself, but I am learning how to accept myself as I am." He stuffs a forkful of macaroni and cheese into his mouth, chews and swallows. "Sorry," he says. "I didn't mean to rant."

"Not a problem," says Paul. "I suspect we have three more rants coming."

"Actually, no," says Deena. "My Parkinson's progression was slow. It took a while to be diagnosed. It was like I had become used to strange things happening to me, and the diagnosis just put a name to it." She takes a sip of water. "I'm not saying that I was fine with what was happening, but there was a degree of acceptance with the diagnosis. A kind of thinking, so now what? I think my ex-husband had a bigger problem with what was going on than I did."

"Interesting," says Albert, "in that I had a much bigger problem with my diagnosis than my ex did. There were tears and anger. He was all, 'We'll work through it.' I was all, 'No we won't.'" He pauses as if ruminating on his upended relationship. "I'm over the tears and anger. I mean they don't change or solve anything. Now I'm kind of blasé about it. Mind you, being in remission sure helps!" At that, there is laughter. "You, Paul?" Albert says.

"You know, I asked the question, but now I'm not sure I want to answer it." He sniffs and wipes at his nose. "Is it okay if I pass?"

Albert reaches across the table and pats Paul's hand. "You're better than you were," he says softly. "Even if you don't feel like it today."

"Amen to that," says Bolton.

"Agreed," Deena nods.

"Thanks, folks."

They all begin to eat their macaroni and cheese again, in contemplative silence.

Chapter Five

Paul Amil is dreaming that he is painting. He is painting the side of a barn with broad strokes. At first, it does not appear to be a picture, but then he sees a picture emerging. Abstract stripes in black, red, yellow, and blue on the side of the barn glowing in the sunlight. Then the barn collapses. Struggling to climb out of from under the collapsed but colourful rubbish, Paul wakes up in a sweat.

*   *   *

Bolton is up before dawn and working diligently to finish off Santali's candle website. Deena comes into the living room and sees him hunched over his laptop.

"Can I make you a coffee?" she asks.

Bolton looks up. "Morning. Would be wonderful, if you are making one for yourself."

"Putting a pot on for everybody." Deena moves about the kitchen putting the coffee on and pouring herself a glass of orange juice and a bowl of Cheerios.

Albert comes into the kitchen. "Smells like morning is brewing." He gets a glass and bowl out of the cupboard.

"Ready to heal walls, if I can borrow your phraseology?" Deena asks.

"I dreamt of taping drywall last night," Albert laughs. "Even plastering it. But more importantly, how did your video blog go?"

"It went well. Focused on renovation 101, tools for beginners. I got a bunch out of my van so I could show folks the basic tools they'd need to get started. Need to do a bit of editing, but will email everybody the link once it's online."

"And done!" exclaims Bolton. "Speaking of emailing, I have to contact Santali."

"Such enthusiasm. He hasn't even had a coffee yet," Deena says with a chuckle.

"Were you up working all night?" Albert asks.

51

"Late last night and then early this morning," Bolton answers. "Well worth it. Santali's candle website is live, but nobody knows about it and it's not registered with search engines. I'll email Santali a link so she can comment on it before we launch."

"Send me one too. I haven't officially hired you to do my website. I want to see your work in action," Deena laughs.

"And send me one too," chimes in Albert.

"Me too," says Paul stepping out of his room and twirling his cane Charlie Chaplin style. "What are people sending to whom?"

"Santali's candle website is live. Deena and Albert are going to give me some feedback."

"I'm in," says Paul.

Bolton hits a few keys. "It's on its way." He then closes his laptop, places it on the coffee table, and rolls into the kitchen to get a glass and bowl from the cupboard. "You folks are fantastic," he says sitting at the table and pouring himself a bowl of Shreddies.

Deena puts a cup of coffee beside Bolton and places one on her place mat as Paul and Albert take seats at the table, coffee and bowls of cereal in hand.

"Just curious, who is doing what today?" Paul asks.

"We're healing basement walls," says Albert.

"I'm working out, training for a race somebody talked me into competing in."

"You?" Deena turns to Paul.

"Mulling over a talk somebody talked me into giving. Working on an article for a client. And maybe even doing some painting."

"Well then," Deena says raising her coffee mug in a toast. "Let the day begin." The roommates all clink their mugs together in celebration of a new day.

*   *   *

Bolton heads to High Park and rolls up the huge hill that is Centre Road, feeling the burn in his arms as he does so, He reaches Colborne Lodge Road and races around it on the bicycle path several dozen times, then rolls like a maniac down the Centre Road hill. He is out of breath and sweating rivers, but his arms feel pumped. "Every day until the wheelchair race tryouts," he chants to himself. "Every day until..."

He returns home and rolls his chair into the bathroom and uses the grab bars to get out of his chair and on to the shower bench. He has a long, warm soak, dries himself off, hauls himself back into the chair, and rolls into the bedroom to put on fresh clothes. He then rolls into the living room, picks his laptop off the coffee table and checks his email. There is one message from Santali with a lot of heart emojis. She loves the candle website. Bolton smiles and replies, telling her that he is waiting for his roommates to give him some feedback and then he will go live with the site and start to promote it. With Santali's comments reinforcing his confidence, he starts to work on Deena's website.

*   *   *

Deena and Albert pick up drywall, drywall tape, plaster, and other essential paraphernalia from Home Depot, and then head to the basement renovation site. They haul their supplies into the basement and clean off the existing concrete block walls as best they can with the shop vac. They do a final cloth dusting down before taking exact measurements. Once measuring is done, they cut wood to build wall frames and then start framing the walls so they can put up the drywall.

Albert stops by a basement window. "I hate to say it, but I suspect water leaks through here. Look at the discolouration of the brick and floor below the window. That's water damage. It might take a while, but without reframing this window, and sealing it to keep the rain out, your wall will go soggy here."

"Good catch," says Deena as she looks at the window. "You are a godsend. Let's stop for lunch and make that our priority after we eat.

"Lunch?" says Albert. "I forgot to pack one this morning."

"I know," says Deena rifling through a paper shopping bag. "That's why I have extra salads, sandwiches, and coffee."

"Godsend meet godsend," laughs Albert as he accepts a couple of Tupperware containers with salad and sandwiches from Deena.

Chronic

*   *   *

Paul is in his room staring at his painting. He squirts red on his palette, picks up a brush, and creates a lopsided, jagged red splotch on his canvas over much of the background. The red splotch is working for him, but he feels something is missing. He knows that the best thing he can do is walk away from the painting until it calls him back.

He opens his laptop and does some preliminary Google research on how young entrepreneurs think. After a while, he heads into the kitchen to make himself a peppermint tea. He returns to the bedroom with his steaming mug and looks at his picture again, briefly. He turns his back on it, fires up his word processor, and reviews the assignment details of an article, how to motivate independent contractors, that he is writing for a construction management trade magazine.

"This is a one-word article," he says. "Money." But he has to write 900 words on the topic.

He turns to look at his picture. Black and yellowish would go with the red, he thinks. Black should work like a force field that has been trying to contain the red. The yellow, with the background bleeding through, should work like, he can only think of one word, cancer. Early-stage cancer trying to consume the red. He pulls out a tube of deep black and one of light yellow. He takes out his palette and several brushes of different widths. But he does not dab any paint on his palette. Instead, he puts down the paint and brushes and picks up his cup of tea. He takes a sip and spits it back into the cup.

"My gosh," he says. "What did I make?" He thinks that he might have made a cup of tea using some strange flavour one of his roommates has purchased. He puts down his cup and picks up his laptop. "Nine hundred words. You can write this in your sleep. Get a shitty first draft done and then maybe you can paint." He lifts his fingers over his keyboard and begins to type.

After finishing the first draft of his article, Paul decides he's too tired to paint. He checks his email messages. One from Nadir confirms the date, time, location, audience, and overall theme of his talk. One from Bolton has a link to Santali's website. He clicks on the link and looks over the website. After doing so, he hits reply to Bolton's email. He pauses and does not reply. He closes his computer and heads into the living room where Bolton is working on Deena's site.

"Got a minute?" asks Paul.

Bolton saves his work, looks up, and nods.

"I was going to email you feedback on the candle site, but figured it's easier to chat."

"Chat away."

"First off, I love the site. The design, images, colours, and writing. It's easy to load and place my order, at least as far as I can tell. I loaded your shopping cart with candle purchases, but didn't place the order."

"I suspect I can get you a discount," Bolton laughs.

"That's almost exactly what I was going to ask. What kind of incentive can Santali offer to motivate sales, to motivate people to buy? This is retail. People want to save money, or get something for free--free shipping or a free package of special birthday candles on orders over $50. That kind of thing."

"An incentive! Marketing 101," Bolton exclaims. "What a great idea. I love it and suspect Santali will too. She's at work right now, but I'm going to email your thoughts to her. She's always checking her email when on break. And as for your candle order, if you have time, feel free to place it. Right now, orders are only coming to me. Credit card processing is not live. I'll delete the order once it arrives. You can tell me if there are any problems."

"You're on," says Paul. "It's a huge order. Enough candles to burn down the house."

*   *   *

After lunch, Deena and Albert seal around the window. Then they begin to frame the walls, getting them ready for the drywall. Deena lifts and places the drywall. Albert hammers it to the frame. "When we have the drywall up, I'm going to need you to tape it," says Deena. "If I do the taping, we shall have jagged and ragged tape lines."

"Not a problem," says Albert.

They hear somebody on the stairs calling down. "Hello?"

"We're down here," Deena shouts.

Harold comes down the stairs. "Just wanted to see how you are progressing or if you need anything."

"All is going well," says Deena.

Harold notices the fresh work around the window. "That wasn't part of the contract."

"It was leaking and needed doing, so we did it, no charge," says Deena. "Thank eagle-eye Albert here."

Harold looks closely at the seal. "Nice job. Since you're not charging me, I'll call it a freebie for my customers."

"I was hoping you'd drop by because I wanted to chat with you face-to-face about something," says Deena.

Albert, knowing what's coming, excuses himself. "Time for a bathroom break."

Harold nods, "Nice catch on the window."

"Not a problem," says Albert.

"I'm all ears." Harold looks at Deena.

"This is a bit difficult to say. One of my roommates is building me a website and if it works out, I may have business independent of you."

Harold shrugs. "I'm sure you do work for other contractors."

"One or two," says Deena. "But you've been my main man for over three years. This would put us in competition."

Harold laughs. Deena looks at him quizzically.

"Do you know how much work there is in the city? I suspect we'd be lucky if we competed on one or two jobs a year. I do a lot of larger jobs, the kind of things I don't ask you, a three-person crew, to quote on. If you are looking for testimonials for your website, write one up about how damn good you are and sign my name to it."

"Seriously?" says Deena. "You're okay with it?"

"More than okay. I'll still be asking you to quote on jobs for me. In fact, I was wondering when the little bird would flap her wings." He pauses. "And I don't mean the British bird, as in female."

"Thanks," says Deena with a chuckle.

"And that Albert guy. I wasn't sure of him at first. I can be kind of macho, as you've pointed out, and he definitely is not." He looks at the work around the window again. "I'd suggest you keep him working with you."

Albert comes back into the room. "Glad you seem to like the window work," he says.

"I've seen better," Harold says with a smile and pauses. "But not much better and not that often."

Deena and Albert laugh as Harold heads back up the steps.

"Sorry for disappearing, but I figured you two could use some privacy. How did he take it?" Albert says.

"He wants us to continue to quote on jobs for him, and he's giving us a freaking testimonial," Deena says as her phone rings. She holds up a finger asking Albert to hold on a second and answers her phone. Albert hears her say, "Tomorrow.... Cool.... I'll have some priming and painting for you to do. I'll text you the address." Deena hangs up and says, "Reggie. He needed today off but wanted to know what he could do tomorrow. After you tape, plaster, and sand, he'll be ready to prime and then paint. We have another job for Harold, a job that all three of us don't need to work on, and Bolton will have my website up and running soon."

Albert beams. "Whatever you say, boss!"

*   *   *

The roommates sit down for dinner, a cauliflower soup that Albert has made. Paul takes a sip of water and immediately spits it back into his glass. "Folks, I think the water is off." He sniffs at his water.

"Mine smells okay," says Bolton.

"As does mine," says Deena.

Paul sniffs his water again. Mine smells okay, but taste it.

Bolton and Deena each take a sip. "Tastes fine," Bolton says and Deena nods.

"Try the soup," Albert says to Paul.

Paul tries the soup and grimaces. "Sorry, Albert, I'm going to have to pass on your soup."

"But it's delicious," says Deena. "I'll have your bowl too."

Albert passes Paul some unbuttered bread. "Take a bite."

Paul bites. "My gosh! Awful."

"You've just self-diagnosed."

"What do you mean?" Paul asks Albert.

"The water, soup, and bread are fine. Your taste buds are off."

"The tea." Paul gets up and runs into his bedroom. "Somebody taste this."

Bolton volunteers. "Peppermint. Cold, but tasty."

"It doesn't taste like crap?" Bolton shakes his head. "Damn," says Paul, "It is me."

"You feeling okay otherwise?" asks Albert.

"My normal self. Tingles, tiredness, occasional fatigue. Nothing different."

"Maybe, just maybe, this is a new MS hit. See what it's like tomorrow. If need be, call your doctor."

"But in the mean time, what do I do about food?" Paul asks.

"I'm a nurse, not a doctor, but I'd say since there are no other symptoms, you either choke down your food or go on a fast."

*   *   *

The next evening, just before the roommates start to prepare dinner--Bolton is making chicken wings--there is a knock on the door to the flat. Paul answers it. "Hey, Martha. Come on in. How can we help you?"

"Was wondering how things are going, and wanted to talk to Deena a bit."

"Things are going well. Having this flat furnished has been a godsend, as is having it renovated for the disabled. Only one of us is in a wheelchair, but I think we all benefit from the lower counters and cupboards. And we're all taking advantage of the mobility bars in the bathroom. Nice to have something to hang on to when you're showering."

"I'm so glad to hear it. When Mike passed away, this house felt empty, even though there were still two of us living here. We never used the first floor. When Genevieve finishes university and gets a job I'm sure she'll want to get on with life, which leaves me here with first-floor tenants that I will hopefully get along with. Like you folks."

Deena comes out of her bedroom. "Wings smell great. Hot and delicious," she says.

"Hey Deena," Martha calls. "Was hoping to chat with you."

"You two take the couch," Paul says. "I'm going to help Bolton, even if the wings are going to taste like crap to me."

"What can I do for you?" Deena asks as she takes a seat.

Martha sits in the char across from her. "You park in the back and may have noticed the back porch in need of repair."

"That I have. I take it Mike never used it."

"We never got around to renovating it. I was wondering what it would cost to replace it with something that would make the back entrance as wheelchair accessible as the front, and create a useable porch."

"Considering what we're paying for rent, I'd say Albert and I could do it for the cost of supplies."

"You're paying close to market value for this place."

"Still…"

"Tell you what, I'll give you money for supplies and you come up with a figure for your labour. I'll deduct that amount from the rent."

"I guess that sounds like a fair deal. I'll take a closer look tonight and email you something later."

"Sounds like a plan. And beyond that, how are you doing?"

"A bit wobbly. But able to do my thing. Have to confess…" Deena raises her voice. "Albert has been a great find."

"Hey, you two," Albert calls as he walks into the kitchen. "No talking behind my back."

"Nothing being said that you wouldn't be proud of," smiles Martha.

"Why don't you stay for wings," Bolton calls out. "I've made far too many. If Genevieve is home, call them down too."

"I don't want to intrude."

"No intrusion. The more, the merrier," says Deena.
"If you are sure then, I'll call Genevieve. Thanks."

During dinner, folks are talking about TV shows and movies that they've enjoyed. Genevieve says there is seldom anything good on, even though they have cable. "You know, it's like fifty channels and nothing on. There are times that I just need to vegetate, but want to do it with something intelligent, or at least half-decent, on the tube."

Bolton laughs and Genevieve looks at him, trying to figure out what's so funny. "I'm not laughing at you," he says. "You're the youngest one in the room, maybe five years younger than me."

He pauses as Genevieve gives him an inquisitive look.

"Have you ever been to sea?" Bolton says, and his roommates laugh. Genevieve looks at him blankly. "Pirate! You read about programs on IMDB or Rotten Tomatoes, look at their rating, and then pirate what you want."

"Isn't that illegal?" asks Martha.

"It's what you might call a grey area in Canada. It's not against the law, but I suppose Hollywood studios could file a civil law suit against a downloader. But you don't need to download. Give me a list of shows that you'd like to see and they will magically appear on a USB stick for you. You can watch them on your computer or connect your computer to your flat-screen TV if you want to watch them on a larger screen."

"Sounds interesting," says Genevieve.

"Might you be able to put *The Handmaid's Tale*, *Big Little Lies*, and *The Undoing* on the stick?" Martha asks with hesitation. "As you know, we don't have Hulu or HBO as part of our cable package."

Bolton pumps the air three times with his glass of ginger ale and says, "Done, done, and done!"

That evening, after the roommates have eaten dinner and Martha and Genevieve have headed back upstairs, Bolton says, "I'll work on your website in the morning, Deena, and then go to High Park to race against the clock. I think I'm getting in some semblance of shape for the wheelchair race tryouts."

"You may be in a wheelchair, but you are the fittest looking of us," says Albert. "Which is to say I could lose fifteen pounds."

"You'd be skin and bones," says Deena.

"Thank you, ma'am. Very kind of you to say so. Not true. But very kind."

"With Bolton's race in mind, the talk for Canada One is confirmed." Paul says. "I get to speak for thirty minutes to motivate a group of young entrepreneurs, Canada One clients, attending a business conference the bank is sponsoring."

"Albert and I will start renovating a living room and dining room combination tomorrow," says Deena. "I quoted on the gig and we got the job. I'm not even sure that Harold took any other quotes. Guess he had a price in mind and we met it."

"It's going to be fun healing walls," says Albert.

"And Martha wants a quote on rebuilding her back deck. She'll deduct the fee from the rent," Deena adds.

"Should just be from what you and Albert pay," says Paul.

"From the full rent," says Deena. "You can make Caesar salad for a week and Bolton can make dessert, and we'll call it even."

Chapter Six

Paul Amil is dreaming of drinking coffee, cups and cups of it, pots and pots of it, gallons and gallons of it. His belly expands and his bladder fills. He wakes up in a desperate need to pee...

*　　*　　*

Bolton is in the living room working on his website. He is trying to decide if he wants a picture of himself on his website, and if he does, if it should be a headshot or a picture of him in his wheelchair.

Paul shuffles into the kitchen to make coffee and get himself some breakfast. He is soon joined by Deena and Albert.

From the living room where he is working Bolton calls into the kitchen, "Can I ask you folks something?"

"Shoot," says Paul as he fills the kettle with water.

Deena fills her bowl with cereal and milk and joins Albert at the table. They both look toward Bolton.

"I'm trying to figure out if I should put my picture on my website. Let's face it, there are some people out there who would not want to work with a black person."

"Would you want to work with somebody who didn't want to work with you because of the colour of your skin?" asks Paul.

"No. But I wouldn't mind surprising them." The roommates laugh. "And if I put up a picture, would I use a headshot of me or one of me in my wheelchair?"

"A headshot would be more professional," says Albert.

"But you in your wheelchair might land you work with companies that have programs in place to do business with the disabled, not that I think of you in that way," says Deena. "But if there is money to be had..."

"A professional headshot might generate business for you within the black community," says Albert.

"Doesn't it all boil down to who you are and what you want to achieve?" asks Paul. "Then you take the best route to getting there." He pours himself a cup of coffee and sits at the table.

"You're saying think about what I want to accomplish, before setting out to do it?"

"Precisely. And who you want to be doesn't just have to be about business. Although it can be a business decision. It can also be about values, community, anything that is an important part of you."

"Which still leaves me not knowing which type of picture to use, but at least now I can think about the what and why."

"It's interesting," says Albert, "In many ways, you are the healthiest of us all, and yet your issue is the most visible."

"Issues," Bolton replies. "If you count my wheelchair and my race. I am no longer a black man who runs. People seem to expect black athleticism."

"But you are a man who builds fabulous-looking websites," says Deena.

"If this is strictly business, you've found what you want to focus on. The person who builds fabulous, and effective, websites," says Paul.

"So that's what my site should focus on, with my headshot, so that potential clients can see it in my eyes. And if somebody does not want to work with a black man, screw him."

"Amen to that," says Deena. "Kind of like if somebody doesn't want to hire me because I'm a woman. They could end up paying more for less of a job."

"Because you are a mighty fine builder who offers reasonable rates," says Albert.

"And has a mighty fine helper who works for next to nothing," says Deena with a grin.

They all laugh, and then Bolton says, "I need to see Santali to get my hair cut, and then get a headshot taken."

"If interested, I can take your picture," says Albert. "I'm a bit of an amateur photographer, or was before I got sick. I've got a decent camera."

"Nurse. Builder. Photographer," says Deena. "You're a regular renaissance guy."

"I write, too. Fiction. Bunch of short stories published in various literary magazines. Writing has been sitting in the back seat, although I have started to ruminate on something."

"Time to move it to the front seat, with you as the driver, no?" asks Paul.

Albert shrugs. "The brain is a bit fuddled from the chemo, making it difficult to sit in front of my laptop and write. Then I take my CBD oil and go to sleep."

"So CBD helps you sleep, but also helps you avoid things you want to do?" Paul says with a questioning voice.

"I guess you could put it that way."

"Maybe I should avoid it," says Deena.

Bolton wheels toward the front door. "Tell you what," he says over his shoulder to Albert. "You can tackle my picture in a couple of days, after I get my haircut."

"My picture too, for my website," says Deena.

"Motivation to pick up my camera. Now I need motivation to move from rumination to writing."

"What you do, and when you do it, I'm discovering, is up to you," says Bolton as he turns his wheelchair towards the kitchen. "Not always easy. Put in the effort and the outcome can be amazing. Speaking of which, I have to go wheel up a hill at High Park and then race around a road. Otherwise, I won't make the wheelchair racing team!" With that, he heads out.

Deena and Albert finish their breakfast and head out to work on a renovation job. Paul sits at the kitchen table for a while, doing nothing, which is all he has the energy to do. "One more coffee, no matter how bad it tastes," he says. "Maybe that will do the trick and let me get my day underway."

*　　*　　*

Deena emails a quote for the back deck to Martha, which she accepts. She and Albert buy the required wood for the deck and begin to work on it, mostly in the evening after finishing their renovation work for Harold. It's not difficult work and it goes well. One evening Bolton wheels into the back yard. He sees Albert starting on a foundation not far from the elevated deck. "If you don't mind my asking, is that where the wheelchair ramp will end?"

"You got it. Fully wheelchair-accessible deck to and from our patio doors."

"You and Deena are the builders, but it seems, and I'm just eyeballing it here, that you will be creating a fairly steep ramp. One that I'd hesitate to roll up. And I'm sort of athletic."

Albert takes a step back. "I see what you mean. Let me get the boss to look at it." He calls Deena over and the two builders confer for a couple of minutes.

Deena turns to Bolton. "Good catch," she says. "I'd like to say that my fingers slipped when I was calculating the angle and I punched in a wrong number, but I think my brain screwed up on this one."

"For what you folks are saving me on rent, happy to help," Bolton says with a smile.

A few days later, the deck is almost done. Over breakfast, Deena says she and Albert will stain it that night. Paul asks if the stain by the patio doors is for the deck.

"It is," says Deena.

"When you get home tonight, if it's okay with you, the deck will be stained," says Paul

"You sure you're up to it?" asks Deena.

"Hey, if I can paint a picture, I can stain a deck," Paul laughs. "It is something I've done before, so I promise it will be done well."

"Then I'm cooking dinner tonight," says Deena.

"I'm helping," Albert laughs.

"Sound like a plan," says Paul, who feels happy to stain a deck rather than work on his picture, at least for a day.

*   *   *

After dinner that night, Deena's phone beeps. She looks at it and then types a reply to the text she has just received. "Going upstairs to help Genevieve understand Greek literature."

"Say hello to them and their mom from us," says Paul.

"Will do."

"I'll be emailing you a link tonight to your website. When you have a moment, give me some feedback on it. I won't go live until I hear from you," says Bolton.

"After I work with Genevieve, I'll look at it!" She heads out the door to go upstairs.

"What did Santali think of the incentive idea to motivate candle sales?" Paul asks Bolton.

"She loved it. Thought it made so much sense. Spend $50, you get free shipping. Spend $75, you get free shipping and a free 10-pack of regular birthday candles. Spend $100 and you get the shipping and a 10-pack of bees wax birthday candles."

"Sounds good. Hope it helps candle sales."

"The site promotion starts tonight."

"This might seem like out of left field," says Albert as he starts to make tea, "but do you ever feel lucky?"

"How so?" Paul asks.

"If we were living in a developing nation, not able to make money, with poor to non-existent healthcare..."

"If you want poor healthcare, or no healthcare, all you have to do is move to the United States," says Bolton. "I have relatives there who pray they never get sick."

"My point, exactly," continues Albert. "We have a solid healthcare system, which the government pays for, out of our taxes, with which I don't have a problem paying."

"And many countries, not all countries, have next to nothing when it comes to healthcare, or they have a rather expensive healthcare system," says Paul.

Albert looks at Bolton. "If I can ask, what did you pay for your post-accident hospitalization?"

"Hospital stay, including operation and meds while in the hospital, didn't cost a cent. The Assistive Devices Program helped with the cost of the wheelchair. I had to pay part of that, but I had assistance."

"If you were American, you'd be in debt for the rest of your life," says Albert. "Same with my cancer treatment. Cost me next to nothing. I paid for a couple of optional items that I had in my room. That was it."

"I agree with what you are saying, but if I may ask, Albert, where are you coming from with this?" asks Paul.

"Ruminating further on my book idea."

"Fact or fiction?"

"That's part of what I'm ruminating on."

"Cool," says Bolton. "Now I have a website to promote."

"And I have a painting to stare at."

"And I have a book to ruminate on."

"You know," says Bolton, "I cannot believe how much TV I'm not watching. Not that I'm complaining about not watching. But I swear I'm going to take a day off soon and binge the heck out of something."

"Keep me in mind," says Paul.

"I'm in," says Albert.

*   *   *

Upstairs, Deena sits with Genevieve in the living room. Martha brings her a cup of tea and says, "I'll check my email and leave you two at it."

Deena toasts her with the mug, "Thanks for this."

"So," Genevieve asks as their mom heads out of the living room, "where do we begin?"

"I was just going to ask you that," says Deena. "Who are you studying and what are your issues with what you are reading?"

"To start with, I believe ancient Greece would be an almost pre-literary society, and yet these authors were writing plays that were popular with an audience that couldn't read or write. The audience almost seemed to worship what transpired on the stage. In each tragedy that I've read, there seems to be action taking place by a few specific characters, in a specific place at a specific time, all cheered on, or commented on, by the chorus. How does the chorus advance the development of the main characters and the action, while not moving it out of time or place? And why were the heroes who strove for greatness frequently brought down by fate, rather than the action of the play..."

Chronic

"Okay," says Deena, "we have a lot to cover. I'll just grind some rust off the Greek literature part of my brain, and I think we can have a great discussion based on your issues."

Genevieve laughs, opens their notebook, and says, "I'm listening."

"You'll be talking too, thinking and talking."

With that said, the two of them begin to delve into the what and why of Greek literature, placing it in context to ancient Greek thought and the overall evolution of literature.

As the evening draws to a close, Genevieve asks Deena if she'd consider conducting a session for her next study group. "It would be so helpful.

"I don't want to step on your tutorial leader's toes," says Deena.

"I was thinking of inviting the tutorial leader to the study group. I discovered that he's a PhD student studying classic English literature. Evidently, he got bumped from the tutorial he was supposed to conduct into this one. I'd ask him if he was up for it."

"Okay," Deena laughs. "Keep me posted. But when you talk to him, don't make me feel like a threat. Just a former PhD student who likes to chat about ancient Greek lit."

"Roger that," says Genevieve.

*   *   *

Bolton takes a final look at Santali's website. "Are we ready to sell some candles?" he asks the air around him. "If so, let's help the search engines index you and help candle lovers find you."

He places his fingers above the keyboard, opens the Chrome browser, and begins to type.

*   *   *

Albert is in the bedroom, lying on the bed, back propped up by a couple of pillows and laptop open on his lap. He doubles clicks on the Word icon to open his word processor. He pauses for a moment, hits the centre icon, and begins to type.

"Sick," he types. Thinks for a moment and adds an 'o'. "Sicko." He has a tentative book title, but he is not sure it is the right title. He puts his index finger to his lips and contemplates the word, thinking about the true meaning of Sicko. He hits the backspace key with one finger repeatedly, deleting the word. Then he types, "*Not A Hundred Percent*." He nods and hits the enter key twice.

"Fact or fiction?" he muses in a low voice to himself. "Or fiction based on facts that I did not think were possible?"

He smiles and begins to type.

*   *   *

Paul is in his room, staring at his painting. It seems to be staring back at him, almost like a reflection in a mirror. He shakes his head. "It's you or draft two of my article."

He picks up a dry paint brush and brushes at his canvas. "There. There. And there. That's where the black would go. And there too. And the yellowish. Bubbling up there, there, and there. And blue diving in from all four corners of the canvas." He puts down the brush. "I don't know." He picks up his laptop and sits on the edge of the bed, the computer on his lap. "Second draft is calling," he sighs.

*   *   *

His hair freshly cut and shaped into a mini-Afro, wearing a short-collar light-blue shirt with a black sweater, Bolton is sitting in his wheelchair under a tree in High Park. Albert is snapping photos. Deena is behind Albert, waiting for her turn to pose.

"After I shoot you both here," says Albert, "I want to go to the top of that hill and try some shots with no background other than sky. And then I'd like to head down to Grenadier Pond and try some with water in the background. When we get home, I'll take some less formal pictures with Bolton working on the laptop and Deena repairing a faucet or painting a wall."

"Sounds like a plan," says Deena.

"I'm taking headshots, keeping your chair out of the pictures to begin with, Bolton, but I'll take several at each location with your chair as part of the picture. That way, you'll have them should you decide to go in a different direction. Deena, I think you should have your tool belt on in every shot, but I'll take some headshots too. In short, you will both have lots of shots from which to choose."

Bolton smiles. "This is so good of you."

"This is me, if you'll excuse the expression, getting back on my feet." Bolton laughs out loud, grinning from ear to ear, as Albert snaps away. "I love that look!"

*   *   *

Several weeks pass. Paul has not done much more than paint the background of his large painting because of article deadlines. He laughs at himself thinking that the motivational speaker needs motivation, but he is pleased to be working on more articles for clients since his speaking business is non-existent.

Bolton is promoting the heck out of Santali's candle website. He knows it can take a while to move people from looking to buying. He makes a few tweaks on her site to motivate visitors to shop. He also finishes and starts to promote Deena's website.

Deena, Albert, and Reggie continue to work on renovation jobs. Deena creates more renovation video blogs. Albert is writing his book, slowly, but moving forward with the story.

The roommates have started to take the occasional evening off to watch British television shows that Bolton has downloaded.

Paul asks Bolton if he can find the movie, *100 Meters*. Based on true events, a Spanish man with MS attempts to finish an Iron Man competition even though he is told that he could not run one hundred meters.

Bolton finds it and the roommates watch it together one night. There is not a dry eye in the house.

*   *   *

For his first one-year check-up, Bolton is in the doctor's waiting room. The receptionist calls his name. He rolls up to her

70

desk. "Room four," she says, "and Dr. Friml will be with you in a couple of minutes."

Bolton rolls down a narrow hall to room four. He backs into the room so he can face the doctor's desk. In a few minutes, as promised by the receptionist, Dr. Friml enters the room. "How are we feeling today," he asks as he takes a seat.

"Not bad," says Bolton.

"Any changes to discuss?"

"Not any that I'm aware of."

"Your bone density tests have come back positive. How is your state of mental health?"

"I've moved into a new flat with three sick but solid roommates. They have various challenges, but work hard. I've found that very motivating. I'd say other than some evening depression, you know before falling asleep, I'm actually doing quite well. Much better than I was when first adjusting to my new reality."

Dr. Friml nods. "Glad to hear that." He plugs his stethoscope into his ears. "We're going to check your heart and breathing, then take your blood pressure."

He does what he said he was going to do. "All seems fine," he says. "Other than your legs, you are in good shape."

"And my lack of erections."

"That too is an issue, one that most likely will not change due to the nature of your injuries." He opens the file on his lap and thumbs through the pages. We have tried medications, constriction bands, and even a vacuum erection device..."

"You know," says Bolton, "it's not an issue anymore. There are things I can do, and am doing, and things that I can no longer do, and now accept that I am not able to do them."

"Your mental attitude has progressed greatly."

Bolton smiles. "You either get on with it, or you don't."

Dr. Friml nods. "Then we will see you next year. But if anything new occurs, if anything bothers you, call and make an appointment."

Chapter Seven

Paul Amil is dreaming. He is dreaming of having his picture taken. Bulbs are flashing all around him. He tries to duck and cover from the flashing lights, but they somehow manage to find him and continue to flash until he wakes up in middle of the night darkness…

*   *   *

For dinner, Bolton makes a grilled cheese for himself. The others are in their rooms napping or working on personal projects. But they slowly start to come into the kitchen.

Paul is yawning and stretching. "Came to just in time to make myself some dinner," he says.

"How are your taste buds?"

"Improving. Not everything tastes like crap anymore. Some things taste a bit off but many things taste somewhat better. Sweet stuff is kind of funky."

"No dessert for you!" laughs Bolton.

"I've cut back on everything, including dessert. Lost ten pounds without trying, not that I'm complaining about the weight loss."

Deena enters the kitchen. "I've made another video blog to link to from my website. That makes three," she says to Bolton. "At the end of each one I make a see-more statement and give my YouTube channel address where all the videos are located, so if people want to see more of what I have to say, they can surf on over."

"Sounds good," says Bolton. "I'll add the link and the photo you've chosen. It's cool, the way you look like you are modeling your tool belt, ready to work with the drill in your hand. We should soon be ready to go live."

Albert enters the kitchen, sniffing. "Something smells good."

"I felt like something informal tonight. If anybody else is interested, we have enough bread, butter, and cheese for all to make grilled cheese sandwiches. We have ketchup too, and fresh tomatoes. I like to add a bit of tomato to my grilled cheese. I can do some shopping tomorrow for more bread, butter and cheese, and anything else on the shopping list."

"I'm in," says Albert. "I'll slice the cheese if somebody wants to butter some bread and slice some tomatoes."

"Got the bread and butter right here," says Paul.

"Taste buds working okay?" Albert asks.

"Not perfect, but somewhat better. Thanks."

The three roommates go to work preparing a grilled cheese dinner when Bolton's phone dings.

"Incoming email," he says. "I've finished eating so I'll check it on my laptop in the living room." He rolls out of the kitchen as Paul places a sandwich in the frying pan that he had heating on the stove. Albert pulls several plates and glasses out of the cupboard and sets the table. Deena places a plate with sliced tomatoes on the table as Albert takes a seat.

Bolton, on his computer in the living room, shouts, "Holly crap. Holly crap! I don't believe it."

"Everything okay?" asks Albert as he jumps up.

Bolton looks up from his laptop. "I've got to call Santali. We have a freaking candle order! A big one, too."

Paul and Albert cheer as Deena runs into the living room. "High-five!" she says and air high-fives Bolton.

"Define big," shouts Paul.

"Twelve, count them, twelve, dripless, scented candles. The ones with a kind of wavy, psychedelic colouring. Premium stock. I'm calling Santali." Bolton pulls his mobile phone out of his shirt pocket and hits a few keys. His friends hear his side of the conversation.

"You've sold twelve candles… Yes, twelve, an even dozen… I have the e-order right here… The psychedelic ones, dripless, scented… I'll give you the details… It came to me because I wanted to make sure the system worked first… Email it to you? Duh, of course… Yes, free shipping and free birthday candles… You don't have to figure out the incentive. It's part of the order. I'll email it to you and set up the system so that we both get orders so I can monitor it… The money should be in your PayPal account. Do me a favour and check before you ship the candles... You have to make them first? ... No, you don't owe me anything... We'll see how it goes over the next couple of months, and then revisit it... No, you don't contact the client. The system automatically sends out a confirmation email and copies it to me... Yes, I'll set it up so it goes to you too... Crap, you're in business... All you have to do is make and ship the candles... But check the payment first..."

Bolton looks at his friends who are sitting at the table, grilled cheese sandwiches on plates in front of them, looking at him instead of eating. "Excitement over," he laughs. "You can eat now."

"Bugger that," says Deena. "When does my site go live?"

*   *   *

That night, Bolton finishes Deena's website and shows it to her. "I like your picture," he says. "You're standing tall, tools at the ready. With the drill in your hand, you look like a gunslinger."

"This is so cool," says Deena. "Even if it doesn't bring in any business."

"Let's hope for requests for quotes. People will be able to fill in the form on your site, click submit, and you will receive an email with information on the job they are seeking and their contact information."

"Cool. No rush, but when will it be live?"

"Do you approve the design and content?"

"I do!"

Bolton clicks a few keys. "You are live on the web right now. And with a few more clicks, you will be in all the major search engines."

"It's live? Now? On the web?"

"Don't worry," says Bolton. "The excitement will wear off. Soon you will be complaining about the lack of visitors and the lack of requests for quotes."

Deena laughs. "Still, it's cool to be out there."

"With a bit of social media promotion and having the site served up to searchers, who knows?"

"Gunslinger, eh? Hadn't thought of that."

*   *   *

Deena knocks on Albert's bedroom door.

"Come in," Albert calls. He is hovered over his laptop typing away.

"Do you think I could try some CBD oil? I think the launch of the website has me kind of revved up. It's like saying that I am, that we are, in business."

Albert puts down his laptop, opens his bedside table drawer, and pulls out a bottle. "It has a dropper and I'd suggest three or four drops. See how that goes."

Deena takes the bottle from him. "With water or straight up?"

Albert laughs. "Shaken, not stirred," he says, in his best Sean Connery as James Bond voice.

"Seriously," says Deena. "I've never done this before."

"Three or four drops in a glass with a bit of water, swirl it around, and chug it down," says Albert.

"I'll do it in the kitchen and will be back with your bottle in two shakes."

"No rush," says Albert, laughing.

*   *   *

Another motivational article complete, Paul looks at his painting. "I guess it's a choice between writing the talk I didn't want to do or continuing to paint the picture even if I have no idea what it's about." He squirts some black on to his palette and picks up a brush. He steps back from his painting, visualizes where he had stroked with the dry brush, and begins to slash on the black.

After painting for a while with black, he squirts some yellow on his palette and then picks up a clean brush and dabs yellow in several spots over the red. Then he adds some magenta, almost as if it is fighting the yellow. And then he uses his blue, has it streaking in from the four corners of the canvas, but not penetrating the red because the black is holding it back.

Chronic

He steps back, contemplates the painting, and adds a bit more black. Then he picks up his magenta and adds more outside the red in places where the black is restricting the red.

Percolating inside him, he feels a kind of inner peace. His tingles seem to diminish in intensity. Then fatigue overwhelms him and he lies down on the bed. As his head hits the pillow, he sees his picture off-kilter and, before succumbing to fatigue, has a final, mundane thought: brush and palette clean up tomorrow.

*　　*　　*

Around noon the next day, Deena and Albert are out renovating. Bolton is racing in his wheelchair around High Park. Paul is sitting on the couch tapping away half-heartedly on his computer, working on a motivational article for a retail magazine when there is a knock on the door to the flat. He gets up and opens the door to Martha.

"Have you got a moment?" Martha asks.

"For you, any time. Come in and have a seat."

When they are sitting, Martha explains that she has a new group of women coming into the shelter where she does volunteer work. "All of them are escaping abusive relationships. Some of them don't have a lot of education, although we get college and university-educated women as well. I get to welcome them to the shelter and am supposed to give them a kind of pick-me-up talk. But I'm so tired of what I see. It's never-ending and it's like I don't know what to say to them anymore." Martha breathes deeply and stares at the floor.

"What tends to happen to other women who have come into your shelter?" asks Paul.

"Most find a job and get their own place. Some make friends with others in the shelter and move in with them. But it takes time and energy and work, and everybody is so depressed and angry, so beaten down to begin with."

"Then that's what you tell them. What you just told me."

Martha looks up at Paul. "What? I tell them that they are beaten down?"

"Exactly. You acknowledge their pain and the reasons for it. You tell them that it's not fair and that you understand the depression and anger their situations have caused. Then you tell them about women who have come through the shelter. Where they are now. How they have made friends, found jobs, found places to live. Moved their lives back on track. You tell them the truth, that it's not going to happen overnight or even in a week. But if they want it to happen, and work on making it happen, it will happen."

Paul pauses and takes a breath. "The shelter, the shelter staff, and volunteers are there to support them on their journey. That it is a journey, of a thousand steps, and that it leads to a new life, a better life, a brighter life. Tell them that the journey itself is rewarding. It's them moving forward. Then you invite them to hold hands and take the first step together. You walk around the room with them. You literally walk around the room holding hands."

"Holly crap!" exclaims Martha. "You really are a motivational speaker!"

"All I've done," says Paul, "is tell you what you just told me. But sometimes we have to have another person say what we have said so that we can hear it."

"I do hear it. As will the new intake. Thanks." Martha gets up and she and Paul elbow bump and laugh. "Air hug," she says, throwing her arms around herself before she leaves the flat.

Now if I can only motivate myself to write this article, Paul thinks as he lifts the lid to his laptop and opens the article file in his word processor. He places his fingers over his keyboard and, after a brief pause, begins to type.

When Bolton comes back two hours later from his race around High Park, Paul has almost completed a solid first draft of his article.

Chapter Eight

Paul Amil is dreaming of racing Bolton. Bolton is running. Paul is in a wheelchair. Bolton is running backward and is ahead of Paul who pushes and pushes the chair's wheels. The chair slows down every time he pushes. Bolton is running on the spot, no longer moving forward. But Paul still cannot catch up, try as he might, until he wakes up fighting for breath and rubbing his upper arms, which feel strained...

*   *   *

A week after her website goes live, Deena races into the kitchen, laptop in hand, where Paul and Albert are eating an early breakfast. "A hit. A palpable hit."

"You been stabbed?" asks Paul with a grin.

"Where's Bolton?" Deena asks. "I've got a request for a quote from my website! I want to kiss him and make sure I'm replying in the right manner."

Bolton comes rolling into the kitchen. "Did I hear that right? Am I getting kisses?"

Paul and Albert laugh out loud.

Deena is so excited she almost drops her laptop. "Okay, I have to put this thing on the table."

Bolton opens the fridge door, and then closes it, taking nothing out.

"No juice?" asks Albert.

"Nervous stomach," says Bolton. "Sorry Deena, I'm racing today so I'm a bit distracted."

"No problem," says Deena. "I have a request for quote in my email in-box. Do I just reply to it?"

"Reply or call however the prospect asked you to get in touch," says Bolton, clearly still distracted by his upcoming race.

"Right, it's here, a couple of lines down. A phone number beside the word 'contact.' This is so cool." Deena races into the living room, sits on the couch, and pulls out her cell phone.

78

"Shouldn't you wait until, I don't know, maybe nine o'clock, before you call?" asks Albert.

"Crap," exhales Deena as she put down her cell phone. "You're right. Although builders are often up early, like us."

"Is the request from a builder?" Albert asks.

Deena scrolls through the message. "Nope," she replies. "Homeowner. So, I should read the full message before taking action?"

"Sound like a plan," says Albert, as Paul and Bolton laugh.

"Trust me," says Bolton, "your excitement will pass. This simply becomes another way of talking about doing business. For instance, Santali no longer emails, texts, or calls me every time she gets a candle order."

"Too busy making candles?" asks Paul.

"That's part of it," says Bolton. "If candle orders pick up, she's going to start working part-time at the hair salon so she has time to make candles in larger batches and fill orders."

"It's going that well?" asks Deena, looking at the time on her cell phone.

"She is racing to keep up with orders, so yes, that well."

"Speaking of racing, what time do we head to the competition site?" Paul asks Bolton.

"We leave in an hour, if you still want to come down with me."

"You're going to be in the audience when I speak. I'm going to be on the sidelines when you race."

"I opened my entrepreneurial account at Canada One Bank several days ago and was given my official invitation to your talk. Now all I need to do is to get my website up and start making some money."

"Your site is not up yet?" asks Deena.

"You know how a shoemaker has no shoes? Well, this website creator has no website. But I'm getting there. Slowly. But getting there."

"Speaking of slowly," sighs Deena as she looks at the time on her phone again, "I swear time has stood still since the request for quote arrived."

"Let's go to the job we're doing for Harold. I bet Reggie is already there. You know how time flies when you're working," says Albert. "Besides, if you call them right at nine o'clock, they'll think you're desperate for work."

Deena's phone pings. She looks down at the screen and taps a couple of buttons. "Holly crap, another freaking request for quote!"

*   *   *

Bolton and Paul take Wheel-Trans to the arena at Ryerson University where the wheelchair races are taking place. They disembark, head into the arena, and find Bolton's racing chair, one that has been lent to him. Paul helps Bolton move from his chair into the racing chair and keeps Bolton's chair in one hand as he balances on his cane with the other.

Bolton straps himself into the new chair. He spins it around and pushes it forward and then back a few feet. "I feel like I have four on the floor," he says with a laugh, "and can't wait to get out of first gear. I'd love to be able to afford a chair like this."

"More candle sales and some renovation gigs, and who knows?" says Paul. "I presume you get to try it out before you race."

"I've got about an hour to run around with the chair on the track. Just don't want to exhaust myself before the race."

"You go have fun. I'll take your four-wheeler and find myself a seat."

*   *   *

Deena, Albert, and Reggie are tearing down a crooked fence that is busted up in places. It's the first step before they dig new fence-post holes and start to build the new fence. Deena is particularly clumsy, dropping her hammer and crowbar, and tripping over ruts in the lawn.

"We should get Harold to talk to his client about flattening this lawn and laying new sod," she says. "Something we could do."

"Good idea," says Reggie. "Something I could do after the fence is up, if the client gives us the go-ahead."

Deena drops her hammer again trying to pull a nail out of a board. The nail seems to want to stay in place.

"Okay," says Albert, "you are distracted and I know why. It's now nine-fifteen. Go call your prospects or you will get nothing done well today."

"It's the shaking," says Deena. "It seems to be particularly intense today."

"Then have a seat and make your calls," Albert says. "Reggie and I can dismantle the fence. Talking to your prospects will calm you down, and that should help diminish the shakes."

"You tell her, Dr. Albert!" Reggie cheers.

Deena tosses her hammer and it hits the ground with a thunk. "I'm going to sit in the van and make the calls." She heads off to the van, almost tripping over a rut on the lawn.

Once his mom is out of earshot, Reggie says, "I've never seen her so worked up."

"I've seen this before. She is like a patient without a diagnosis. Anything could be wrong and that scares the crap out of them. Once they get the news--cancer, I may die, but at least I know what's wrong with me--they tend to settle down. She's launching a new business. We all want it to succeed, but it has her name on it so she's carrying the weight. Give her a couple of calls, and she'll start tackling this like the pro she is."

"Kind of like how she stopped taking sexist crap from Harold, but it took her a while to blast him because he was the prime source of her income."

"I knew Harold was a bit of a macho man but didn't know he was that extreme."

"He is and he isn't. He has to mirror his clients. You're macho; I'm macho. That kind of thing. But mom's not macho. Once he figured out what mom was like, he settled down."

"You're only sixteen, eh?"

"Yep. For three more months."

"I think you'll do well at this if you choose not to go back to school."

"Hey," Deena calls from the van. "Can you two handle the fence? I've got two on-site potential renovation meetings to attend."

"We got this, mom."

"Hear the confidence in her voice?" asks Albert. "She has her diagnosis."

*   *   *

After trying out his racing chair, Bolton is talking to Paul who is sitting in the stands. "The chair is so cool. It's nothing like my chair. An hour isn't much time to get used to it, but it really rips."

"You looked good out there. Almost like you knew what you were doing," says Paul. "What's the plan?"

"There are like twenty of us trying out for thee spots on the Toronto team. Initially, there will be four heats, five racers in each heat. Top three in each race move on to the next round. That gets us down to twelve racers. Then three heats with the top person moving on, which gets us down to three. Then one race with top two making the team and competing against teams from other cities in Ontario to pick the Ontario team that competes at the Canada games."

"And from there, on to the Paralympics?"

"It's a long haul, but yes."

The two friends sit silently for a moment before Bolton says, "You know I'm going to try my best to make this team, but if I don't..."

"I tell Nadir that I can't do the talk," Paul laughs and then pauses for a moment. "Hey, you've taken amazing steps to get here and you've created two websites, both of which are generating business. If I dropped out of the talk now, I'd be a prime asshole. You race. I speak. No matter your outcome."

"I can't thank you enough for helping me get back on track."

"And it all started with you motivating me, the motivational speaker."

*   *   *

After speaking to two homeowners, Deena comes back to where her son and Albert are working on the fence. They have the old one torn down and cleared out of the way, and have started to dig new fence-post holes. Waving a cheque in front of her, Deena says, "We have a marvellous second-floor deck to build. Here is the advance for supplies."

"Way to go, mom."

"All right! You're in business."

"And I have to quote on a major kitchen renovation. Have to get some figures from a kitchen cabinet-making company and an electrician. If we land the gig..."

"Fingers crossed," says Albert.

"Listen guys," says Dena, "I feel like I've deserted you here."

"Mom! We've got this covered."

"There's a lot of fine work required, the kind that gives you issues. Reggie and I work well together," Albert reassures Deena.

"Still..."

"Still nothing," says Reggie. "You're getting us work and making us money."

"Look," says Albert, "if it makes you feel any better, haul the rest of the new fence wood out of the van, and then go gather the information you need to put your quote together. You've got us a new deck, now go land us a kitchen!"

Deena gives Albert and Reggie each an air hug. "We're going to do this." She takes off to the van and hauls the wood for the fence into the backyard. Once that is done, she makes calls so she can get some quotes from a cabinet-making company and an electrician she has worked with.

*　　*　　*

In his first heat, Bolton finishes second so he gets to move on to the next round. Paul cheers madly for him. In his next heat, he finishes first and gets to move on again. During a break in the action, he wheels over to where Paul is sitting. Paul comes down from the stands.

"You did well. Second and freaking first, moving on in both instances."

"Thanks," says Bolton. "I've seen this in sprinting. Each heat, folks get faster and competition becomes more intense."

"You dig deeper."

"I dig deeper!"

In the next heat, Bolton digs deep and finishes in second place. His arms are on fire as he crosses the finish line.

"Final heat," Paul says under his breath. "Final Toronto heat."

But that's where Bolton's stamina runs out. In the final heat, he finishes in third place, with only the top two making the team.

Paul pushes Bolton's wheelchair towards the area where the racers are congregating. He sees Bolton engaged in a conversation with a man who seems to be peppering him with questions, so Paul stops a short distance away. The man hands Bolton a business card and they bump elbows. Bolton waves as the man walks away and Paul pushes the wheelchair forward.

"You did so well," Paul says.

"But not well enough."

Paul helps Bolton move from the racing wheelchair into his chair. "It's like you are moving from a Maserati to, I don't know, Deena's work van," Paul says. Bolton laughs. "You came damn close."

"But we weren't playing horseshoes."

"Still." Paul pauses. "If you don't mind my asking..." They move away from the area where the two winning racers are celebrating. "Did I see a guy give you a business card?"

Bolton wheels his chair towards an arena exit. "I'd like to head home and shower."

"Not a problem," says Paul.

"And yes, a guy gave me his card. Coach Kay, the coach of the Toronto wheelchair basketball team. Says he's looking for somebody fast and nimble to patrol an outside lane and he's holding tryouts in a few weeks. Told him I only played house league basketball in high school, well before the accident. He says he's got shooters lined up and that he needs defensive speed. If I make the team, he says, I can learn how to shoot from the chair."

"And?"

"Told him I'd think it over."

"So we're heading back down here in two weeks?"

"I don't know. If he finds somebody fast who can shoot, it will be another tryout that goes nowhere."

"Your racing tryout didn't go nowhere. Look at what you accomplished today. Look at the sweat on you. I mean, honestly, how do you feel right now?"

"I feel... fine. Great, actually. I did my best. Gave it my all. My arms are in the best shape they've ever been in. I'd be an idiot if I didn't keep on racing in High Park, just for the fun of it."

"Kind of like how you built Santali's website."

"How do you mean?"

"You're good, but did you think you'd be good enough that she'd have to cut back on her hairdressing hours so she could make the candles she's shipping out?"

"Not really."

"But you had fun, you both had fun, building her site."

"We did."

"That, my man, is life. Have fun. Sometimes it pays off in unexpected ways. Sometimes there is no payoff. Either way, you've had fun."

Bolton rolls up the exit ramp. Paul opens the door out of the arena. The two of them move into the sunlight. Bolton looks up at Paul. "What you're saying is that I should have fun trying out for the basketball team, do my best, and don't give a hoot about what happens? If nothing happens, move on to whatever. Because trying beats sitting at home feeling sorry for myself. Something like that?"

"I can't tell you what to do or how to feel. But for me, that kind of sums it up."

"But what about you and the talk you didn't want to do?"

"Oh, I wanted to do the talk. Trust me. My fear is that my body won't let me do what I want to do."

Bolton waves down a cab. Paul helps him into the back seat, folds up his wheelchair and puts it in the trunk. He slides into the back beside Bolton.

"You know, if you told me that your body won't let you do the talk, I wouldn't think less of you, at least not now, for backing out."

"I'm a part of a two-day entrepreneurial conference. I told Nadir that my body might not let me do the talk, but I was willing to take that chance if he wanted to take a chance on me. He has a backup motivational video in place, a good one that I recommended. If I can't do the talk, he plays it and then the entrepreneurs move on to the next segment of their conference. In other words, I'm on, unless I can't go on."

"And you're coming back down here in a couple of weeks with me?"

"To see you try out for the basketball team? You bet I am."

Later that day, Paul calls Nadir and asks him for a favour.

"I can do that," says Nadir. "Give me a day and I will get back to you with the details."

"Thanks," says Paul. "I appreciate it. Bolton will freak, but he'll appreciate it too."

*　　*　　*

A few days later, on a Saturday, Deena heads down to the University of Toronto to meet with Genevieve's Greek literature study group, including the tutorial assistant. The assistant, Marty, is standing outside the classroom when they arrive. Genevieve introduces Deena to Marty.

"Mind if we talk for a second before going in?" Marty asks Deena.

"Not at all." Deena nods to Genevieve who enters the classroom.

"Genevieve tells me you are a Greek literature PhD," says Marty.

"Was a Greek literature PhD student. Didn't complete my degree."

"I'm an English literature PhD student, bumped from my early English literature tutorial assistant role by union rules. Somebody up there..." Marty waves at the ceiling. "...said we needed a TA for a course that has Greek in front of literature. They said that I'd be teaching first-year students, so it shouldn't be a problem."

At this, Deena rolls her eyes. "Ah, life at university. I had almost forgotten how insane it could be," she commiserates.

"I needed the job, so I took on the TA duties."

"You're doing well with it. I did a one-on-one with Genevieve. The basics are there. You're conducting a literature tutorial. It's more like the Greek historical context is missing. If it's okay with you, that's what we can focus on today, the historical context and its impact on the literature."

"Sounds lovely. I'm looking forward to it."

"Tell me your phone number and I'll text you the names of two books you can use to get a handle on the historical context and, quite frankly, teach from."

"It's 4-1-6..."

Deena tries to enter the number into her phone but has difficulty hitting the keys because of tremors in her hands. "Tell you what," she says, "after class, I'll give you my phone number. You call me and I'll save your number when it shows up on call display."

"Genevieve told me about your Parkinson's."

"Always a workaround... Shall we go in then, and begin?"

"After you. And thank you for this."

"It will be fun."

The study tutorial goes well. When it moves out of areas of history, how the ancient Greek writers treated their audience and how the audience reacted to what they saw on stage, and into areas of literature, Deena lets Marty speak. They are delighted to find themselves team teaching. When the tutorial ends, Marty elbow bumps Deena and says, "Your leaving was the university's loss."

"And my gain," Deena replies, before giving Marty her cell phone number to call.

On the way home on the streetcar, Deena says to Genevieve, "That seemed to work out. Marty is a knowledgeable fellow."

"He was different today. Almost like your being there made him more confident."

"Hope the rest of the year goes just as well, but not to change the subject..."

"Which means you are about to do so."

"If you don't mind my saying, your mother mentioned that you are non-binary."

"That I am. Non-binary, asexual. At school, guys hit on me. Lesbians hit on me. I even had a gay guy tell me that he found me oddly attractive," Genevieve says with a dry laugh. "But my body doesn't respond to anybody. Even in high school, I was a wallflower."

"Not being sexually active doesn't make you a wallflower. Different than many of your peers, maybe, but not a wallflower. Life is long and complicated, but it's also over, historically speaking, in the blink of an eye."

"So where does that leave me, while I'm sorting me out?"

"Find your interests, your passions, which I sense you are doing. Engage in them, in what gives you joy. That is what you do."

"But I really don't know what that is."

"Good, you have something to do. A quest. Go seek it out. It doesn't have to be anything that makes you rich or famous, but something that enriches you and makes you feel fulfilled. Even searching for it can be engaging." Deena sits back in her seat. "Would you like a metaphor?" Genevieve nods. "Think of yourself at the buffet table of life, tasting all that it has to offer. One day you might find a dish that is particularly to your liking. It becomes your staple."

"I take it from your life, you can even change staples."

"From classical Greek literature to home renovations. I don't regret my studies one iota, but it was time to change dishes. I don't regret my marriage. It gave me a wonderful son. My husband and I decided to change dishes, and I found myself a new plate. There are so many avenues to travel and different dishes on each one." Dena laughs. "I think my metaphors are getting mixed, but you get what I'm saying."

"School is pretty tasty right now. But what I eat next, or to continue the mixing, where I travel next, I don't know."

"Exactly." They get off the streetcar and walk the remaining blocks home in silence, each ruminating on their thoughts. At the door to the house, Genevieve gives Deena a double air hug.

Chronic

"Thank you for today, for all the avenues and all the dishes," Genevieve says with laughter and appreciation in her voice.

Later that evening, sitting on the living room couch, Deena says to her roommates, "I had fun today. I conducted a tutorial on Greek literature and had a long philosophical chat with Genevieve. When I got home, I applied for several jobs."
"What?" exclaims Albert.
"I'm not going to give up the renovation business. It remains my life's blood. I am thinking of trying a new dish, so to speak. Teaching continuing education courses. One night a week."
"Greek literature?" asks Paul.
"Home repair and renovation. Several high schools and colleges offer such courses and I've applied to see if I can teach one."
"Renovation and teaching renovation," says Albert. "If you land a course, you can bring me in as a guest lecturer for the class on the different ways to hammer nails. Straight or on an angle!" He pauses. "Pun intended."
Paul and Bolton laugh as Deena says, "You're on, my man. You're on."

* * *

The next day over breakfast, Paul is eating his cereal while typing on his laptop.
"This is unusual," says Deena as she enters the kitchen and starts to make her breakfast. "You at the table with your computer, eating and typing."
Albert and Bolton enter the kitchen and start to pull out bowls, spoons, and glasses.
"I got into the Facebook MS support groups I belong to first thing this morning. I usually do it after breakfast because I get engaged in the messages and time just flies by. This morning I'm engaged and hungry."
"I've looked briefly at the cancer groups, but didn't join any," says Albert.

89

"I'd never say you should or shouldn't join," says Paul. "I have a bit more time on my hands. I've found a lot of positive people with MS doing their best, as we all do with our maladies. But every once in a while, you see a post that breaks your heart. People who are debilitated by the disease. In wheelchairs, like you are Bolton, but unable to function much at all. Or you read a message from somebody crying over a break-up, like you had Deena, but with partners who are downright cruel, accusing them of faking their disease. Or you read a message from a younger person whose family members are telling them it's all in their head."

"What do you do when you read posts like that?" asks Deena.

"Often I reply and say, 'Tell your partner that you have been faking. Faking being well, which is much harder to do than faking being sick.' Or I say, 'Tell them that they are right. That you have the MRI results to prove that it's all in your head, and down your spinal cord too.'"

Paul's friends laugh.

"What kind of reactions do you get?" asks Albert as he sits down with his juice and cereal.

"The replies get a few thumbs up and a few happy faces. I mean there is nothing I can do for these people, other than maybe help them smile for a few seconds before they try to sort out the miserable conditions that surround them."

"It gets to you, doesn't it," says Deena. "Things are not as depressing in the Parkinson's groups, but then I don't go into them very often so I could be missing the worst of it."

"It's why I had to leave the cancer groups. Not that people are having personal issues with family or partners. However, the posts there were so raw and painful that they actually made me feel healthy, which I am more or less right now, knock on wood," says Albert. "I guess I started to feel guilty about being in remission."

"I don't belong to any paraplegic groups," says Bolton. "Call it my way of being in denial."

"Each of us has to find our way to deal with our issues," says Paul. "I've always seemed to be able to reach out to people for some reason. Heck, I married a therapist, someone who reaches out for a living. I guess it's just part of who I am."

"You reached out to me," says Bolton. "I wouldn't have a website business and wouldn't be trying out for the basketball team, if not for you."

"I really didn't do anything, other than help you hear what you were telling me you wanted to do. And besides, who got the person who had retired from public speaking to sign up to give a talk?"

Bolton chuckles. "Yeah, I guess I did do that, didn't I?"

Chapter Nine

Paul Amil is dreaming. He is dreaming of standing in front of a large crowd that he is supposed to be talking to. Instead of talking, he is painting on a large canvas. He paints two lines up and down the canvas. Crosses them with two lines. Paints a large 'X' in the centre of the crossing lines. He looks at the crowd, which cheers him on. The cheers are so loud that they wake him. He feels oddly content.

*   *   *

The next day, over a dinner of fish, rice, and broccoli that the friends have all pitched in to make, Albert shouts, "Recap! Everybody describe how their day went. I go first." He scoops more broccoli onto his plate. "I finished building a fence with Reggie. We work well together. We work hard together. It's a mighty fine fence. Tomorrow, we stain it. Why didn't I say I built it with Reggie and Deena? Deena, your go."

Deena chews and swallows a mouthful of fish. "Did you mention my name because you want the others to think I was slacking off?" she laughs. "I converted one email request for quote into a deck-building job. I need to do a bit more research before I quote on the other request. And earlier this evening I received another request for quote from the website. Bolton, I'm going to have to ask you to back off promoting my site until I get a bit more organized."

"I haven't been doing squat to promote your site the last while, so search engines are now driving traffic your way." He continues. "I was focused on trying out for the wheelchair racing team. Made the final heat before crapping out, as you know."

"But..." says Paul.

"But I've been asked to try out for the Toronto wheelchair basketball team, so I have to head up the street to the schoolyard tomorrow to shoot a few hoops, after I buy myself a basketball."

"Sorry about the racing team," says Deena. "But way cool about the basketball tryout."

"Paul?" asks Albert.

"I watched Bolton do well at the wheelchair racing tryouts. I haven't told him this yet, but I called Nadir."

"About your talk to Canada One entrepreneurs?" asks Deena, not sure what Paul means about the relationship between Bolton's race and his call to the bank.

"Canada One is the official bank of the Raptors, Toronto's basketball team in case anybody here isn't sports-minded. Unless he objects, Bolton isn't going to the schoolyard tomorrow to shoot hoops. We're going to the Air Canada Centre, home of the Raptors, to shoot some hoops with a few Raptors before their practice."

"Say what?" screams Bolton. "Are you shitting me?"

"I take that as a yes," says Paul.

"I'm not sure," says Bolton.

"Yes," Paul, Albert, and Deena shout in unison.

*   *   *

After dinner, Deena, Bolton, and Albert are sitting in the living room. Deena is on her computer, working on the kitchen quote. Bolton has started to build his website. Albert has his computer in his lap and is pecking away at his novel, *Not A Hundred Percent*.

Deena looks up from her work and says to Bolton, "I've been meaning to ask you. The work you've done, registering my website domain, building my site, optimizing it for search engines, registering it with search engines, and promoting it through social media. If you were to do this for a corporate client, what would you have charged?"

I did it for you and Santali for no charge, to get some work to link to from my website, and for the lovely testimonials you've both given me."

"I know, and I appreciate that. But if you had charged me?"

"Maybe five thousand dollars."

"Then if you don't mind, that's what I'll pay you, in installments, as money comes in from the website."

Bolton shakes his head. "Not an issue."

"Santali is giving you some money, isn't she?"

"She insisted. We've agreed on a small cut per sale."

"Then that's what I'll do too. Five percent of each job I get through the website until I hit five thousand dollars. If I need more marketing down the road, we'll adjust what I owe you. It only feels right, kind of like good karma."

"She pays me," says Albert, "and I'm going to be making even more money because of you, so if you don't accept payment from Deena, I'm going to stuff bills under your pillow."

Bolton laughs. "Okay then, if you insist," he says to Deena, "But my fee is only two thousand five hundred dollars with my friends' discount. You keep track of what you owe me, what you pay me, and when you pay it. You can e-transfer funds to me. But no rush."

"I swear, if we land this kitchen project, you're getting the payment in full in one transfer."

Paul comes into the living room carrying his painting, which is under wraps, in one hand with his cane in the other. "I just talked to Quelina," he says to Bolton. "She says congratulations on getting the tryout and she has offered to drive us to the Air Canada Centre for the practice with the Raptors."

"Cool," says Bolton.

"If you folks have a moment, I'd like to show you something," Paul says. "If there are no objections, I'd like to hang what I've got here someplace in this room." He leans the painting against a chair and pulls back the wrap so that his roommates can see it.

"Cool," says Deena. "Marvelous colours. Self-portrait?"

"Sorry?" Paul says, surprised by the question. He turns the painting back so he can look at it again. "I guess it's fair to say that there is a bit of each painter in every painting they do, but self-portrait?"

"Yeah I see it," says Albert.

"You guys are shitting me," says Paul.

"The MS is trying to hold you in, but you are breaking free, as I see it," says Bolton.

"And it's boiling up in spots, kind of like lava, a volcano that could explode at any time," adds Deena.

"But you are working to dodge the lava," Albert continues.

"Your health is trying to help you," says Bolton, "but it's being blocked by the MS."

"I see your physical, emotional, psychological, and intellectual health fighting for you, trying to break through your MS," adds Deena.

"You have painted Paul, a decent person dealing with his issues," says Bolton.

"Really? You see that?" asks Paul. He steps back to look at the painting. "What you see… what I have painted… Holly crap, what I have painted is a portrait of all of us."

Bolton wheels around Paul so he can get a better look at the painting. Deena and Albert get up and stand behind Paul.

Deena steps back from the picture. "Yes, it's a group portrait."

Everybody laughs, and then Paul says, "Damn it all, it's more than that. This painting is my talk for Nadir's entrepreneurial conference. I've been painting my talk, not writing it." He picks up his painting in his free hand, twirls around with it, and heads for his room. "Thank you so much. I needed you to see what you saw so I could move beyond what I saw to see more clearly what the painting is saying."

"Your talk? I don't see it," says Bolton. "I see you, and even us, but not a talk to entrepreneurs."

"How is the painting your talk?" asks Albert.

"I think I get it," says Deena. "'Think' being the operative word."

"Tell us," says Bolton, "how is it your talk?"

"You're all going to be at the talk," says Paul. "You, Bolton, in the audience. And you two backstage to pick me up when I fall over."

"If you fall over," Deena replies.

"Which you won't," Albert chips in. "But we'll be there, like your entourage."

Paul pauses outside his room. "You'll hear how this painting is my talk then because I still have to translate it into words."

Painting in hand, Paul returns to his bedroom and closes the door.

"Hey, I thought you were going to hang it in the living room," Deena calls after him.

Paul's voice comes to them from the bedroom. "Sorry folks, it's research now. I need it beside me when I write."

*   *   *

A month passes. Paul's painting has evolved from random colours and designs, to self-portrait, to group portrait, and is slowly becoming his entrepreneurial motivational talk. In addition, Paul still has a couple of articles to write for clients. Bolton continues to promote the heck out of Santali's candle website as his own site is coming together, but is not yet live. Deena, Albert, and Reggie are happily working on a couple of renovation jobs for Harold and on several jobs that Deena has landed through her website.

Deena continues to video blog about renovation and starts a video blog about Parkinson's. Albert's book is moving forward. He had a theme and is turning the book, loosely based on a true story, into a novel. The roommates continue to take the occasional evening to watch television series that Bolton has downloaded.

Bolton asks them if they want to watch *Me Before You*, a movie in which a girl in a small town forms an unlikely bond with a recently-paralyzed man she's taking care of. The roommates have liked Bolton's previous downloads, so they agree to watch it together one night. When the movie ends, there is not a dry eye in the house.

"Maybe we should stick with British police procedurals," says Paul as he wipes tears from his eyes.

*   *   *

Deena is in the doctor's office, Dr. Samsung sitting across from her.

"Your results look good," the doctor says. "The motion and movement tests have shown some diminishment in your mobility and increases in your tremors. Not a lot, but some. Your posture is good, as is your overall strength, and you have no difficulty talking." Dr. Samsung flips through her charts. "Are you still doing your physical therapy, focusing on the balance and stretching exercises the therapist gave you?"

"Every night before I go to bed, and often in the morning before breakfast."

Dr. Samsung nods. "Wish all my patients were as co-operative as you are." Deena laughs as the doctor continues. "I think the exercises have been helping. As I recall, you had a negative reaction to the Carbidopa-levodopa medication, but you seem to be as well as you can be without it."

"The nausea and light-headedness were significant. I couldn't work. I'm doing okay without it. Not doing the finesse work, but can lug fairly heavy material, drive, and talk to clients."

"Well then, come back next year, unless anything untoward happens before then. We'll keep you off meds unless you have specific new symptoms that need to be treated."

Dr. Samsung stands to end the meeting, and Deena stands as well. "Keep well," says Dr. Samsung, offering a fist bump which Deena accepts before leaving the office.

Chapter Ten

Paul Amil is dreaming of playing for the Toronto Raptors basketball team. He tosses the ball. Swoosh. Through his own net. His teammates begin to pummel him. He falls to the floor beneath their blows, but finds an opening in the floor and crawls into it, into the darkness. He wakes up on one side, close to the edge of the bed, feeling dizzy, as if his head is about to explode...

* * *

Not long after breakfast, Quelina comes to the house to take Paul and Bolton to the Air Canada Centre. They go in the entrance Nadir told Paul to take and head toward the basketball court. Three Raptors are on the court waiting for them, as is Nadir. He is standing behind a sleek three-wheeled wheelchair.

Paul introduces Bolton and Quelina to Nadir and Nadir then introduces Paul, Bolton, and Quelina to the three Raptors--Kyle, Jamal, and Fred--who air high-five them in the post-pandemic manner with no hands connecting.

"By the way," Nadir says to Bolton, "Paul said that you don't have a sports chair." He slides the chair he is holding towards Bolton. "Do you want to try this one on for size?"

"I was going to four-wheel it as best as I could today, but this chair looks very cool. Thanks for letting me use it."

"How shall I put it?" says Nadir. "It would be good of you to make the wheelchair basketball team because you now have a sports chair. It's yours, courtesy of the bank."

"Really? I mean... Wow!" exclaims Bolton. He pulls his chair beside the sports wheelchair and lifts himself from his chair into the new one, and straps in. "Fits like a glove. I don't know what to say... Thank you so much."

Nadir awkwardly elbow bumps Bolton and Paul. He laughs and says, "I don't know if I will ever get used to that." Then says to Bolton, "All the best with your practice and upcoming tryout."

Before he leaves, he tells Paul to let him know his audio-video needs for the talk. Paul nods and gives Nadir a thumbs-up.

"So, do you want to shoot some hoops?" Jamal asks Bolton. Paul and Quelina take Bolton's four-wheeler and head for the stands.

Bolton has a good practice, dribbling, passing, and shooting. Then the group breaks into two teams, Jamal with Bolton and Kyle with Fred, and play a half-court game to twenty-one.

Before they start to play, Jamal says to Bolton, "We'll play man to man. You're on Kyle. Nobody in the league dipsy-doodles like him. Just lay back and stay in front of him. Let him wear himself out trying to spin by you."

Paul and Quelina watch from the stands and cheer Bolton on as he tries to keep Kyle away from the basket, failing at times, but frequently succeeding. Bolton even scores several baskets.

As the four are playing half-court basketball, Quelina turns to Paul. "Do you mind if we talk?"

"I'm all ears."

"You know that I'm seeing someone, Martin Hurdle."

"The therapist. You've done some group work with him, yes?"

"Yes, that Martin."

"You know I'm cool with that. We split up so you could get on with your life, rather than become my caregiver."

"I know. It's taken me time to accept that," Quelina says. "Martin and I got together and then we kind of went on hold for a bit. You know therapists, how we have to analyze and reanalyze everything."

"I seem to recall that from our relationship." Paul smiles and Quelina laughs. "Does Martin know that we're friends? Mind you, if that's an issue..."

"He's very cool with it. He's a confident guy, without being smug. And you? How are things going?"

"If you are asking me if I am seeing anybody..."

"No, just generally. Wondering how you are doing."

"I still have MS..." Quelina chuckles and shakes her head as Paul continues. "And since we're opening up here, I have to say that I'm getting worried about finances. I'm not doing any motivational speaking, other than the talk I'll do for Canada One.

The writing doesn't pay well and is kind of drying up. I finished an article recently but I don't have any others due and don't have the energy to market myself the way I used to."

Paul pauses and clears his throat. "We have a good thing going at the flat, but I'm concerned. If I can't pull my weight financially, the whole thing falls apart. And no, I'm not asking for a loan. This is bigger than a short-term fix that I couldn't pay back."

"Well then, I'll tell you more," says Quelina. "Martin and I finished our analysis and are now at the point of taking the next step. We've been talking about moving in together. He knows I'm talking to you today. If I move in with Martin, you and I sell the house. You know it's not mortgage-free, but you'd get half of a decent chunk of change. And if he moves into the house with me, we'd buy you out. You and I would figure out a fair value for the house and you'd get a monthly cheque. Are you financially okay for a few months until Martin and I sort it all out?"

"I am."

"In a few months, you'll either receive a decent cheque or the beginning of monthly cheques."

"You're not moving in together just to pay me off, are you?"

"It's a serious relationship."

"Why do I suddenly feel a whole lot better about things?" Paul looks out over the basketball court. "Go Bolton, go!" He shouts. "You go, guy!"

He and Quelina watch as the Raptors give Bolton a lot of room and let him take the final shot of the game and score the game-winning basket.

"The fix was in," says Bolton with a laugh. He air high-fives each of the Raptors and thanks them for their time and for the experience.

"Didn't anybody tell you, we'll see you tomorrow at one o'clock? You're working out with the full team," says Kyle.

Bolton spins around in his chair. "Tomorrow? Full team?"

"You bet," says Kyle as Paul and Quelina come down from the stands, Paul, walking with a pronounced limp, is using his cane to keep himself as straight up as he can. Quelina is wheeling Bolton's wheelchair to centre court.

"If you come with Bolton tomorrow, we can have our physiotherapist take a look at your knee," Fred says to Paul.

"She's real good," says Kyle as Bolton glances at Paul and Paul nods.

"Thing is," says Bolton, "Paul has MS. It manifests itself in unpredictable ways at strange times."

"Sorry to hear that," says Jamal. "The limp is an MS thing?"

"A lot of people with MS have mobility issues, many are on scooters or in wheelchairs. I use the cane..." Paul holds up his walking stick, "...for balance. Having said that, if your therapist has time and wants to work out some of my kinks, I'd be up for that."

"Sounds good," says Jamal. "We'll definitely speak to her today about it."

"Speaking of speaking about it, we almost forgot," says Kyle. He spins the basketball he is holding on his index finger. "You scored the winning basket," he says to Bolton. "You get the game ball."

"The day just keeps on getting better," says Bolton, and then he asks, "Does it come autographed?"

The three Raptors pat their jerseys as if looking for a pen. Paul turns to Quelina. "You wouldn't happen to have a pen in your purse?" he asks.

She pops it open. "Better than that, I've got a fine marker." She pulls the marker from her purse and hands it to Kyle. The Raptors sign the ball and pass it to Bolton who dribbles it several times.

"And to think, I was going to buy one to practice with. Although I don't know that I want to play with an autographed ball."

"Dribble the hell out of it," says Kyle. "The full team will sign one for you tomorrow. You can dribble this one and keep the new one on your mantle!"

Bolton laughs and bounces his ball on the court. "Can the day get any better?"

Quelina drives Paul and Bolton home. Paul says he's tired, not fatigued, but tired. Quelina says she'll come in, make him tea, and sit with him a bit. Riding his new sports chair, Bolton takes his basketball to a local schoolyard to shoot more hoops.

When they get inside, Paul sits on the couch and puts his head back. Quelina puts the kettle on for tea. "Can I ask you something?" She pulls out the teapot and two mugs.

"Shoot," says Paul, with a weak smile. "Are you going for two points or three?"

Quelina laughs as she plops a mint tea bag into the teapot. When the kettle boils, she fills the pot, picks it up, along with two mugs, and joins Paul on the couch. She places the pot and mugs on coasters on the coffee table. "All this stuff you are doing with Bolton, don't get me wrong, I think it's great, but it's exhausting you."

"And your question is?" Paul asks as he sits up and fills a mug with mint tea.

"Why? You're not well, at least not as well as you should be. Why do you push yourself for Bolton?"

Paul sits back as Quelina pours herself a mug of tea. "I suppose I'm doing it because I can," he says.

"But look at you now. If I said let's go for a walk to High Park, you probably wouldn't be able to get off the couch."

"You're the therapist. Do I have to spell it out for you?" Paul pauses and sips some tea. "I can do next to sweet bugger all. I'm living, in part, vicariously through Bolton. He's a smart kid who has pulled himself up by the bootstraps after making a horrendous mistake. He can do stuff. He deserves what little support I can give him."

At a loss for words, Quelina clears her throat.

"Don't you see?" Paul continues. "It would be a mistake for me to do nothing, even if I can only do a little. What else is a sick, depressed man supposed to do?"

"You're not depressed."

"Be the therapist. Analyze me. Of course I'm depressed. But I still have choices. Sit on my ass all day? Wait for bouts of fatigue to hit? Pass out? Come to? And continue to sit on my ass? Or get on with whatever life I can get on with? Depressed as I am, as bad as I feel, I don't want to, freaking refuse to, sit on my ass and do bugger all."

Paul puts down his mug as Quelina sits silently. "I will not sit," Paul continues. "If MS wants to win, I'm going to make it fight, and battle, and beat the hell out of me before I drop. And when I drop, I'm going to pick myself up, dust myself off, and fight on until I have no fight, nothing, left. MS is not going to beat me unless it conspires to kill me."

"Paul..."

"No, don't Paul me. If MS conspires to kill me, I'm going to laugh in its face and call it the bloody coward that it is. Make me sick. Take me down. Screw you MS! I'm going to paint my paintings, support Bolton as best I can, and give my Canada One talk even if I have to be carried off the stage. I want to show young entrepreneurs that you have to fight if you want to win. That you have to get back up if you get knocked down. That you never surrender in the face of adversity. Change course if required, but that's just a tactic you use in your battle to succeed."

"I'm sorry. I didn't mean that you should do nothing..."

"I know you care, Quelina. You care too much. Thanks for caring, but I'm going to be okay. Because that's what I choose to be. No matter the circumstances. I just couldn't drag you through my battle, because your caring too much would have brought you, brought both of us, down. I will always love you, but it's my battle, my fight, not yours."

"I know. I really do know. I just want the best for you."

"Helping Bolton, living vicariously through his success, is part of the best."

"I see it now. I do."

"Then we're cool?

"We're cool. I just had a moment."

"A caring Quelina moment."

*   *   *

The next day, Albert is out shopping for some house plants. He knows that green is not in the nature of Paul, Deena, or Bolton. They told him that they had no objections to houseplants, but they would never remember to water them.

"Unless you're going to be the houseplant gardener, I'd suggest you buy cactuses or some other plant that needs no water," Bolton said.

"Even cacti need the occasional drop of water," Albert replied with a laugh.

Albert has a cardboard box with five potted plants in it and feels good about his purchases--two colourful crotons, a lemon-lime dracaena, and a gorgeous flowering anthurium.

Beside the plant shop on the main drag is a pet store. Albert watches a kitten playing in the window of the store. The kitten seems to be trying to catch beams of sunlight streaming in through the window. Albert shifts his plant box into one arm so he can push open the door with the other, and enters the store.

*   *   *

Deena comes home to what seems like an empty house. She goes into her room and fires up the video blog and screen capture software on her laptop. She places her laptop on her nightstand and sits on her bed in front of it. She adjusts her webcam so that she is seeing herself in the lower corner of her computer screen. She opens The Parkinson's Canada website in one browser folder and the Michael J. Fox Foundation for Parkinson's Research in another tab in the browser folder. She sets up Chrome so that the Parkinson's Canada website is visible on her screen. She looks at some notes that she has scribbled down on a piece of paper sitting beside her laptop, takes a deep breath, hits record, and begins to speak.

"Some of you may know me as Deena the Renovator." She holds up a hammer in front of her webcam. "Many of you may not know me at all. To both groups, I'd like to introduce myself as Deena, a person with Parkinson's, a complex brain disease, a neurodegenerative disease. Yes, in case you are wondering, it is the same disease that Michael J. Fox has."

Deena clears her throat. "Everybody's Parkinson's journey is different. I'm going to talk about my journey today, but before I do, I'd like you to know that currently there is no cure for the disease. Having said that, you should know that Parkinson's itself does not directly kill those with it. If someone is elderly or weak and they have Parkinson's, they may develop other illnesses, like pneumonia, that could lead to their death. But I am not elderly. I am a renovator. A renovator who has Parkinson's..." Deena glances down at her notes and then continues to speak.

*   *   *

Home again after shooting hoops in the schoolyard, Bolton begins to work on his website.

Deena comes out of her room carrying her laptop and sees Bolton tapping away at his keyboard. "May I ask you something, when you have a moment?"

Bolton looks up from his keyboard and laughs. "When I'm working on my website I pray for interruptions."

"You're sure?"

"Fire away."

"You know how you put links to three of my renovation video blogs on my website?"

Bolton nods.

"Well, I've just recorded my first Parkinson's video blog. It's on YouTube. I don't think it belongs on my business website, but I want to drive traffic to it. Thoughts?"

"Open your laptop and go to your Facebook account."

Deena sits on the couch and does what Bolton has requested. "I'm there."

"See that search bar in the upper left corner?" Deena nods. "Click on it and enter the word Parkinson's." Deena does so. "What do you see?" She scrolls down the search results and sees several Parkinson's groups, which she tells to Bolton. "Join them. Find out what they're about and what they allow you to post. Where appropriate, post a link to your video blog, with a brief description of your talk."

Deena scrolls further down in the search results. "My gosh, look at all the groups!" she exclaims. "This is what Paul does on Facebook, isn't it? Chats in the MS groups."

"He does. So now that you have something to say, you can chat in the Parkinson's groups."

Deena taps away on her keyboard. "I just joined three Parkinson's support groups. As soon as I'm accepted, I'll post."

"There you be."

"I'll join other groups and see what can be posted, and let you get back to building your website."

"Are you sure you don't have any more questions?"

Deena laughs. "Just one, and then your excuse for procrastinating is leaving the living room. How was your practice? And how is Paul?

"Practice was freaking amazing. Look at this." Bolton points down to the basketball beside his wheelchair. "And I have a new sports wheelchair folded up in the front hallway. As for Paul, that guy pushes himself. I think he's asleep now."

"We're good at not comparing symptoms, but I think he's running on the lowest energy of all of us."

"But damn, he does run."

Before Deena heads off to her room, Albert arrives home. He is carrying the plant box in one arm and holding onto a large canvas bag in his other hand.

"Holy crap!" Deena runs to the door. "Let me give you a hand."

Puffing, Albert hands the plant box to her. "Put the plants on the kitchen table, if you don't mind."

"Consider it done."

"What's in the other bag?" Bolton asks.

"Is Paul here?" asks Albert, putting the plastic bag on the floor.

Deena comes in from the kitchen just as Paul limps out of his bedroom. "Did I hear my name being called?" he asks as he scratches his sleepy head.

Albert pulls a plastic box from the bag. There is a cage in the box. "Since you are all here..." He lifts the cage out of the box and opens its door. A small, furry, champagne-coloured head pokes out the door.

"Kitty!" says Paul.

"I'm sorry I didn't ask. I can take him back if anybody is allergic or objects."

"Kitty!" Paul says again moving to the cage and getting on his knees.

"I take it that you're okay with it," smiles Albert. "Deena? Bolton?"

Deena laughs. "Like plants, I have no objection. But I won't be watering it either. Or cleaning the litter."

"Santali had cats. We got along, more or less," says Bolton.

Paul has lifted the kitten, which is champagne-colour with several white stripes, from the cage and is lying on his back with the kitten on his chest, pawing at his shirt.

Albert laughs at Paul. "This box is the kitty litter box. I'll put it on my side of the room and keep it clean. Are you okay with that?" he asks Bolton.

"Not a problem, but I suspect you can put it in Paul's room."

Everybody laughs as the kitten crawls over Paul's face and paws at his hair. "Kitty," Paul gurgles with a kitten's foot in his mouth.

*   *   *

Later that evening, after dinner, the roommates are sitting in the living room. Bolton is taking a break from working on his website and has his headphones on, watching a downloaded TV show.

Deena is promoting her Parkinson's video on various Facebook groups that she has joined and is replying to posts, especially those written by people newly diagnosed with the disease. She already has a dozen likes and hearts on her links to the Parkinson's video. In addition, several people have thanked her for her encouraging, positive, and honest words in the video.

Paul is sitting on the couch, head back, and with his eyes closed, petting the kitten who is purring in his lap.

Albert is on a roll, at his laptop working on his novel. He looks up at Paul intermittently and smiles.

Bolton finishes his TV show and looks at his watch. "Too late to start another episode," he says to nobody in particular. He looks over at Albert. "How goes the book?"

"I'm having fun with it. Doubt that I'll ever find a publisher, but will give away a few PDFs to you folks and some of my friends at the hospital."

"Why don't you self-publish it?" asks Bolton.

"Because I know nothing about that," Albert laughs.

"I've read about it. Doesn't seem all that difficult. It's something I can learn how to do."

"Another reason to not finish your website?"

"Santali is proofreading the site for me tonight, taking a break from candle making. When she gets back to me with her comments, I'll look them over and revise as required. I should be live tomorrow. I can learn how to self-publish for you, and add that skill to my website. You can give me a glowing testimonial and maybe even sell a few copies of your print and e-books at Amazon, Barnes and Noble, Chapters, and Kobo."

"You know," says Albert, "I just might take you up on that. I have to finish the sucker first. Then we'll talk."

"Cool, that will give me time to learn how to self-publish!"

As Bolton and Albert are packing up their laptops, Paul stops petting the kitten and starts to moan lowly.

"You okay?" asks Albert.

"Seem to be coming down with a headache. I'll take some Tylenol and hit the sack." Paul scratches the kitten. "Do you want him tonight?"

"I think you two have bonded."

"But he's your cat."

"He's the house cat. You take him to your room. He knows the litter is in our room, so we'll keep our doors open and he can have the run of the house."

"You're on." Paul winces. "Better get that Tylenol."

Deena's cell phone rings. She looks at the screen. "Crap."

"Problem?" says Albert.

"My ex, Gilbert. Never good news when he calls." She answers her phone and heads to her bedroom for privacy.

That night, while sleeping, Albert bolts awake. He looks around thinking the cat may have jumped on his bed. But there is no cat. Then he hears it, a low moaning coming from outside the bedroom. He gets up, grabs a housecoat, and runs out of the room. Paul is on the couch face down, moaning.

Albert sits on the edge of the couch beside him. "Are you okay?"

"My-my h-h-head," he stutters. "It's sp-splitting apart."

"How bad is the pain?"

"S-s-scale of one to t-t-ten, it's t-t-twenty."

"Uber or ambulance to emergency?"

"U-Uber. Not d-d-dying, but..."

Albert calls for an Uber and gets dressed. When the Uber arrives, Albert helps Paul into the car and asks the driver to take them to Saint Michael's, his old hospital, even though Saint Joseph's Hospital is just down the street.

Albert knows the nurse in emergency on registration duty. He chats briefly with her, tells her that he has done an initial assessment, and fears that Paul may be having a stroke. The nurse sends them directly to the back. "Hate to do that, but we just saved an hour's wait, and if you are stroking..." Albert says to Paul who is leaning against him.

Soon after they get to the waiting room in the back area of emergency, Dr. Fickler, with whom Albert used to work on occasion, comes down the hall and motions them into a room. "I got a call from the front desk saying that you were here with a patient in some distress. Stroking?"

Albert thanks Dr. Fickler and helps Paul onto the examination table. Paul moans and rolls onto his side as Albert explains to Dr. Fickler that Paul has MS and is experiencing a severe headache. "On a scale of one to ten, he says it's a twenty."

Dr. Fickler picks up the phone and makes a couple of calls, then says to Albert, "CT scan to see if he is stroking. If not, a test to determine if it's vertigo. If not, it's could be a bizarre MS symptom."

"Okay if I keep him company?"

Dr. Fickler nods his assent as an orderly shows up with a wheelchair to take Paul for his CT scan.

After the scan, an agonizing wait in a crowded hallway, they learn that the results are negative. No stroke. The orderly and Albert take Paul for his vertigo test. On the way to the testing room Paul murmurs, "It's down to a fifteen." Albert pats his shoulder.

Twenty minutes later, after the vertigo test, they return to the room where Dr. Fickler first saw them, with the test results. Albert helps Paul get up on the table where Paul lies on his back. "Wow, the room is spinning and lights are blinking and flashing in the corners of my eyes."

"Technically, I shouldn't look at this," Albert says to Paul as he rifles through Paul's test results. "Not vertigo." He places the results file on the doctor's desk.

Dr. Fickler returns to the room and looks at the papers in Paul's file. "How are you?" he asks Paul.

"Pain down to fifteen," Paul mumbles.

"No stroke. No vertigo. That's good news," says Dr. Fickler. "Here's what I want you to do. Lie on your side facing me, put your hands together, and tuck them under your head. Inhale through your nose, exhale through your mouth. We're going to give you a half hour like this, and then see how you are doing."

Paul does as asked. Dr. Fickler says to Albert, "I'm going to see some other patients. You okay with him?"

"Not a problem. And thanks for seeing us so quickly."

"I'd like to say my pleasure, but it's never a pleasure seeing people who are not well. Speaking of which, how have you been doing?"

"Doing okay, thanks. Remission. Doing a bit of work. Holding my own."

Dr. Fickler pats Albert's shoulder. "See you in thirty minutes or so."

About forty-five minutes later, Dr. Fickler returns to the room. Paul is sitting at the table drinking tea. Albert is sitting in a chair across from him. "How are we doing?" Dr. Fickler asks Paul.

"Pain down to a ten. Hurts like hell but is almost tolerable. Feel like I can walk even though I'm kind of dizzy."

"We're going to chalk this up to MS, but I'm going to write you a prescription that might help with the pain. I say might because you know MS. Sometimes you have a symptom that seems like one illness but it can't be treated because it's not that illness. In other words, your head hurts but it might not be what we'd label a headache. It's like MS is masquerading as symptoms of an illness that it is not, and won't respond to medication meant to treat the illness."

"Because it's not that illness?" asks Albert, verifying what the doctor is saying.

"It's MS. Just doing its bizarre thing," says Paul. "This kind of symptom-illness confusion has happened to me more than once over the years."

Albert and Paul get home about four hours after they headed out to Saint Michael's Hospital. Deena and Bolton are still sleeping. The kitten is on the couch. Paul stops in front of Albert's bedroom door. "I don't know how to thank you," he says.

"Hey, when I collapse one day, pick me up and we'll call it even."

Paul laughs and heads to his room. The kitten gets off the couch and follows him. Paul almost passes out from fatigue before he can lie down. He comes to an hour later, his head still throbbing, with the kitten on his chest, purring contentedly. He makes eye contact with the kitten. "How did you know that I needed someone to watch over me?"

*   *   *

The next day, Paul and Albert get up late. When they move into the kitchen, they see Bolton in the living room, typing away on his computer.

"Has Deena not come out of her room for breakfast yet?" Albert asks.

"She came out about an hour ago. Said she was heading to Tim Hortons for a coffee and to meet her ex," Bolton says. "You two slept in."

Paul explains what happened.

"I slept through all that?" asks Bolton.

Paul and Albert laugh.

"You sit down," Paul says to Albert. "I'm making you an herbal tea, scrambled eggs, bacon, and toast."

"Spoil me rotten," says Albert. "How's your head?"

"Pain is pretty much down to a five. I'll pick up the meds after breakfast and see if they help."

*   *   *

Deena and Gilbert are sitting in a Tim Hortons drinking coffee. Deena is also munching on a muffin.

"You couldn't think of a better place to meet?" asks Gilbert, with a degree of belligerence in his voice.

"You said you wanted a coffee. Tim Hortons serves coffee," says Deena, remaining calmer than she feels.

"Okay, fine, I don't want to fight you. How goes the renovation work?"

"It's steady. But you'd know that from how busy Reggie is."

"Aren't you going to talk the kid into going back to school?"

"He knows going back is the option I'd prefer that he take. But he's sixteen. It's his choice. What should I do, take him to school? Besides, he lives with you. Aren't you trying to talk him into going back?"

"He lives with me, but we don't talk much."

"Speaking of talking, why did you want to meet today?"

"It's like this." Gilbert takes a sip of his coffee. "My work is not as steady as it used to be. I might lose the apartment and am not sure where Reggie and I would end up. I need some money."

"You need money? When we broke up, you were making twice the money I was making. I don't blame you for breaking up with me. Hell, if you had been sick, I probably would have left you, that's how little love there was left in our relationship."

"Still, if you want Reggie to have a stable home..."

"Sounds like it's you who wants a stable home, at my expense. Reggie can probably afford a small but decent place if you bale. And don't think you can get money from him. Make him pay rent, sure, but don't go digging into his savings."

112

"I don't know what you want from me," Gilbert pouts.

"The same as what I'm giving you. Absolutely nothing. Sweet bugger all."

With that, Deena chomps down on her muffin and puts the lid on her coffee cup. "Don't call me again, unless you have something important to say, which I can't imagine." She gets up and leaves Tim Hortons.

Gilbert sits for a moment and then leaves too, his coffee barely touched.

Chapter Eleven

Paul Amil sleeps through the night with nary a dream. He wakes up feeling fresh and almost healthy, headache all but gone…

*　　*　　*

Over breakfast, Paul says to Bolton, "Time flies when you are having fun, no?"

"What do you mean?" asks Bolton.

"Today's the day. Your tryout for the wheelchair basketball team."

"And you think time has been flying? The last two weeks have been the slowest, most tedious in my life, other than being able to practice two more times with the Raptors."

Paul smiles and shakes his head. Albert and Deena laugh. "But the day is now here," says Albert. "And we'll be there."

"Who? Where?" asks Bolton.

"We. There. At your tryout," says Deena. "Thank goodness it's on a Saturday and we don't have to give up any work to cheer you on."

"You're coming down with Paul? Thanks, guys."

"We're coming down," says Paul. "But your cheering section is going to be bigger than the three of us."

"What do you mean?" asks Bolton.

"Shall I name names?" asks Paul. "Let's see. Albert, Deena and I." He counts three fingers. "And then there is Martha and Genevieve." Moves two more fingers. "Reggie, Quelina, and of course Santali… What do you know? I still have two fingers left."

"I appreciate it, but it's just a tryout."

"I suspect we won't be the only ones cheering on our chosen hero."

Bolton looks at his watch. "I need to leave in an hour."

"Uber is already booked," says Paul.

*   *   *

In the stands, there are several hundred supporters of the wheelchair participants engaged in the tryout. Thirty players are trying out to make the team, including players on the old team. They have to earn their spot on the team once again.

The players are divided into six teams of five players each. "We will not be selecting one team. We will be selecting the best players on various teams," Coach Kay informs them. "However, how your team plays is important, because a good player is a team player who elevates the team."

A round-robin tournament with fifteen-minute games is scheduled. Bolton plays in the second game. The players think the round-robin schedule is random. However, the coaching staff has set it up so that some players will be competing against specific other players. For instance, Bolton will be on the floor playing against Jonathan Grounder, somebody who was previously on the team and one of the most conniving players, with the best three-point shot, of all thirty participants.

The first game is raucous and competitive, with solid wheelchair basketball played. When it is complete, Bolton's team, with red jerseys on, and their opposition in blue, wheel onto the floor. Bolton's cheering section goes wild. Bolton looks up at the stands and sees his supporters cheering him on. He lowers his head and shakes it, but smiles while looking down at the floor.

Coach Kay calls Bolton over to the sidelines, "Look," he says, "the forward you are facing, Jonathan Grounder, is damn good." Bolton doesn't know just how good. "You have speed. We'd like to see you use it to shut him down."

Bolton nods in response and takes his position on the floor opposite Jonathan. The ball is tipped. The blues get it. There is a quick pass to Jonathan who moves forward and then dipsy doodles, which Bolton was not expecting, and breaks into the clear. He moves down the floor, Bolton moving fast behind him but unable to prevent him from shooting. Jonathan goes in for an easy two-point layout. Bolton's cheering section goes quiet, but only for a moment as the reds move down the floor.

Bolton is thinking as he moves down the floor. He remembers Jamal's words about Kyle. "Nobody in the league dipsy doodles like him. Just lay back and stay in front of him. Let him wear himself out trying to spin around you." And it clicks. The game has something to do with speed, as in racing, but much of it is a dance and he has to follow Jonathan's lead. He has to dip when Jonathan dips and doodle when Jonathan doodles. "It's position and speed," he mutters to himself. "When he spins, he has to come out of it to find me right in front of him."

The reds fail to score and the blues take possession of the ball, which is quickly passed to Jonathan. Bolton wheels back and dips and doodles with Jonathan, staying in front of him each time he spins. Jonathan is so frustrated that he passes off the ball. Completing his pass, he cuts for the net, Bolton cutting with him and staying in front of him so he can't take a return pass.

Now that Bolton is using both speed and finesse against Jonathan, he manages to shut him down, other than several foul shots and a couple of layups, for the rest of the game. The two teams see-saw back and forth, the blues eking out a two-point lead over the reds with less than a minute left in the game.

The reds foil a blue invasion and head back up the court with the ball. Bolton is not an offensive player, but he uses his speed to break free of Jonathan. The ball is passed to him as he crosses the centre line. He pulls up just outside the three-point line and fires a shot. The ball is in the air when the buzzer goes and it swishes through the hoop. The referee motions three points and the reds and their fans in the stands, including Bolton's cheering section, erupt in screams of victory.

Jonathan wheels up to Bolton, who doesn't know what to expect. "I don't have a say on who makes the team, even though I was team captain before the tryouts."

"It's only been fifteen minutes and I'm ready to puke from working to keep up with you," says Bolton.

"I hope to see you puking on the team, with me." Jonathan holds out his hand and Bolton gives him an air shake and a smile.

*   *   *

Two days later, Bolton is making lunch when his phone rings. He answers it and a woman asks if she is speaking to Bolton Lewis. He replies in the affirmative, thinking he's been hit by a spam phone call. Then the woman says, "Congratulations on making the wheelchair basketball team."

Bolton is stunned. "Thank you," he says. "I thought I'd hear the news from Coach Kay, but thanks."

"Coach Kay hasn't called? You haven't heard..."

"He hasn't called."

"Oh my, I am so sorry. I didn't mean to... This is so embarrassing. Listen, can you forget what I said. Wipe it from your memory, and let me restart this call. And when Coach Kay calls, pretend I said nothing."

Bolton laughs. "Okay... Hi," he says.

"Hi," says the woman. "Is this Bolton Lewis?"

"It is indeed."

"This is Jenifer James, in public relations with Wheelchair Basketball Canada. Coach Kay said somebody who tried out..." She pauses monetarily. "...tried out for the wheelchair basketball team was a website designer. I guess that is what you put down as your occupation on the tryout form. I've been to your site and found it most impressive, along with the sites you've built. In fact, I am going to place an order for scented candles."

"Santali, who makes the candles, will be pleased."

"The thing is, we've lost our website designer and we've decided to go freelance with our site redesign. I was wondering if you could quote on redesigning the home page and creating pages for each team, including team photos and individual photos of members of each team. We'd take the photos and write the biographies of coaches and players. You'd put it all together. The site is currently a bit of a dog's breakfast."

"Building websites is what I do, so I'd be happy to chat a bit more with you and then submit a quote."

"Great. Glad to hear it. And that other thing I said..."

"Other thing?" says Bolton. "I have no memory of anything other."

Jenifer laughs and they continue their website design conversation.

Over dinner, Bolton tells his friends that he has some unofficial news about the wheelchair basketball team. He tells them about his phone call with Jenifer.

Paul says, "We shouldn't cheer or toast you until you get the official call. But unofficially, congratulations." The friends all toast Bolton and laugh. "And all the best with submitting your quote for the website gig."

That evening, sitting in the living room working on a quote for Jenifer, Bolton gets a call from coach Kay and acts ecstatic, in large part because he is ecstatic, when he officially gets the news that he's made the team.

"Oh, and one other thing," Coach Kay says. "You might get a call from Jenifer James in our PR department. She's looking for a website designer. I suggested that she check out your website."

"Thanks. I hope to hear from her." Bolton hangs up and shouts out, "It's official." He hears "Congratulations" from Albert sitting on the couch across from him, working on his novel, and echoes of congratulations coming from the bedrooms where Paul and Deena are getting on with their lives.

"I've got to call Santali and tell her!" Bolton says as he clicks open his mobile phone's contact list.

*   *   *

A few days later, Bolton's phone rings. He answers it.

"A thousand. I've hit a thousand," a voice screams in his ear. "Santali?"

"Can you believe it? I sold candle number one thousand today, to a Jenifer James. She bought a dozen frigging scented candles!"

Bolton doesn't say anything about Jenifer. Instead, he says, "Congrats, big time. That is so cool." Albert looks up and Bolton whispers, "She's sold candle number one thousand." Albert raises a thumb in congratulations.

"I've made the basketball team and you've sold a thousand candles."

"We have to have a party," Santali says. "At your place. My place is full of boxes of wax and candles and food colouring and candle-making tools. We'll celebrate you making the team and me selling a thousand freaking candles!"

"A celebratory party here? You're on," says Bolton. "I'm sure everybody here will be okay with it, but let me get back to you with the official word." He and Santali say goodnight.

Albert looks up from his laptop, "You've got my okay, as long as I'm invited."

Paul comes limping out of his bedroom, cat in his arms, "Sounds like a lot of excited talk going on."

Deena comes out of her room too. "I sense joy in the air."

Bolton tells them about Santali's candle sales and her party idea. Everybody is in.

"Shall we invite your cheering section from the basketball tryouts?" says Albert.

"Absolutely," says Bolton. "And I want to get a huge, decorative candle-shaped cake for Santali.

Deena's phone vibrates. She looks down at the screen and hits a couple of icons to open her email. "Holy shit," she exclaims.

"What is it?" asks Albert.

"We got it. We got the major renovation job! I need to call the electrician. And maybe turn down the paint job we were supposed to start working on."

"You'll make the calls tomorrow, yes?" Albert laughs.

Deena looks at her watch. "Yes, tomorrow. But early. And Bolton?"

"That would be me."

"You are getting paid in full for the website. In freaking full."

The friends all go to bed, but Albert can't sleep even though he's taken his CBD oil. He gets up and knocks on Deena's bedroom door. "Come in," she says. Albert enters. Deena is sitting up in bed, a book in her hands.

"Am I disturbing you?" Albert asks.

"Was just reading. Guess it's like CBD oil for me. Helps me get to sleep."

"Do you have other people you can use to work for you when I get chemotherapy? I shouldn't start a big job just before my chemo is scheduled. And when I get the chemo, it puts me down for several days, sometimes longer if I have a bad reaction. And you've got this big job coming in, the first of many, I hope. But if I was due for chemo when the job started, I would not be available to work with you and Reggie."

Deena takes a breath. "Worrying about me is keeping you up?" Albert nods. "How sweet!" Albert laughs. "But you're right. It's something I should think about. I tell you what, let's use this renovation job as a test."

"How so?"

"The paint job is just walls and ceilings. In theory, it can be done by one person. I won't turn it down. You'll do it and I'll put together a crew for the reno job. Remember the basement we did, how Harold had another crew working on the first and second floors above us?"

"He had a good crew up there."

"He did, and I got to know some of the guys. I'll call them and see what they're up to. See if I can bring in a couple for the reno job. They'd get along with Reggie. They were impressed that somebody so young worked so hard and so well."

"That could work."

"I'm glad you brought this up. I need to be aware of it and it will help me move into the next stage of my business. I mean if the purpose of the website was to generate business, then I have to be prepared to do the business that it generates. We've been doing well, but we need to be prepared to move to the next level."

"That would be you as a full-time contractor, like Harold."

"I haven't said much, but it's the direction I need to move in. I can't do much of the finesse work and even hauling stuff, the grunt work, is becoming more difficult."

"Oh, Deena."

"Not impossible, don't get me wrong. And some days I'm fine. Strong like bull. But you know, I'd be dumb like jackass if I didn't admit that I am slowing down. It's something that I'm aware of but have been in denial about."

*   *   *

The next morning, Bolton calls Santali about the party. "Everybody is in," he says enthusiastically. "We're making a list of guests."

"That's so nice, but I don't know. I think maybe I've changed my mind."

"Changed your mind? You've sold a thousand freaking candles. That is worth celebrating. I hoped that you might sell like maybe a hundred candles by now, if you were lucky..."

"I know. It's just that..." She pauses.

"Just what?"

"I don't know how to tell you this. I met someone, Justin, about six hundred candles ago. I haven't said anything to you because you've been so wonderful, and I don't know...."

"Santali, I'm so happy for you. Is it serious?"

"It's getting there."

"Does Justin know your website designer is your former boyfriend?"

"He does."

"And does he know we're still friends? At least I think we are."

"We are. He knows."

"Does he know that there is nothing more between us?"

"He knows about your accident and why we broke up."

"Does he hate me or hate the fact that we still talk?"

"No," Santali laughs. "Not at all."

"What's the big deal, then? There's more to life than making candles, cutting hair, and befriending a cripple. You are getting on with it."

"You are one of the least crippled cripple people that I know. I just wasn't sure how you'd react. I mean, I'd like to bring him to the party..."

"Listen, I'm okay with him because you're okay with him and he sounds like he's okay with me. It's that simple." There is a silence that Bolton finally breaks. "So? Are you going to bring him to the party?"

"What's the date and time? And what can I bring, other than Justin and some candles?"

*   *   *

After dinner, Albert asks Paul who is sitting on the couch with his head back and eyes closed, "How's the head?"

Paul opens his eyes and looks over at Albert. "It's been better, but it's been worse. The last few nights, the pain spikes up to a ten. I lie on one side or the other, hands tucked under my head, and it subsides. I wake up at maybe an eight. During the day it might drop to a five."

"Does it ever go away?"

"Not since the first hit."

"Are you taking the meds?"

"Not helping. No side effects, but not doing anything. I'll keep on taking them until I finish them..."

"Google New Daily Persistent Headache. I think that is what you are experiencing. I'm not saying you are going to like what you read, but understanding can sometimes help a little. No?"

"Like when I was diagnosed with MS. 'Ah, that's why my testicles are tingling and I'm seeing spots in front of my eyes.' Doesn't make the MS go away, but at least you know what shit you are dealing with."

"Yeah, something like that."

Chapter Twelve

Paul Amil is dreaming he is on stage, a PowerPoint slide projecting on the screen behind him: "Paul Amil is a Fake Motivator." Light snow begins to fall. Paul looks at the slide, waving his hands at it trying to make it disappear. The snowfall gets more intense. Soon it's a full-blown storm and Paul is buried under drifts. He digs his way out with bare hands turning red from the cold, breaks through to the surface, and sees his slide shining brightly in the clearing sky. He wakes up shivering because he has kicked off his blankets…

*　　*　　*

Albert is in his doctor's office, Dr. Tivoli sitting across from him with X-ray images on the computer monitor behind her. "You're a nurse. I suspect you can see what I am seeing here." Dr. Tivoli points at a slightly blurry image on the screen.

"Would you call that a smear on your computer monitor, something that Windex can eradicate, or a recurrence of my cancer?" asks Albert.

"I would not call it a full recurrence. I'd call it something we need to keep an eye on. It's not the end of your remission, but we wish it wasn't there."

"Increase the chemo intensity and frequency?"

"That's what I would suggest. The hope is we can eradicate this before it starts to spread."

"The fact that it's there, though, means it has started to grow."

"The line I just used about eradicating it works well with patients who have no medical knowledge."

Albert laughs. "But you are not calling it significant?"

"That is true. I'm calling it something we need to attack and watch. As you said, we're going to modify the intensity and the frequency of your chemo and book you for X-rays in three months. Then we'll talk."

"I will see you then, in three months.

Chronic

*   *   *

A month passes. Paul's large painting is complete. His entrepreneurial motivational talk is not. He hasn't written more than a couple of paragraphs, and he is not pleased with what he has written.

Bolton is in serious training with the wheelchair basketball team. The team is invited to the occasional Raptor's practice and is even given tickets to a couple of games.

Deena, Albert, and Reggie are working on renovation jobs that have come in through Deena's website, although Albert has to take days off now and then when his chemo sessions drain his energy. When that happens, he stays home and works on his novel. Deena's hands shake more often than not when she tries to do fine motor work. But she can still drive the van and lug material. Reggie works as her foreman on some jobs, hiring labourers and skilled trade people to get various jobs done.

The roommates continue to take the occasional evening to watch British television shows that Bolton has downloaded.

Albert asks Bolton if he can find *The Bucket List*, a movie about two terminally ill men who escape from a cancer ward and head off on a road trip with a wish list of things to do before they die. Once again, at the end of the movie, there is not a dry eye in the house.

"Maybe we really should stick with British police procedurals," says Albert as he wipes tears from his eyes and blows his nose at the end of the movie.

*   *   *

It takes a while to arrange the celebration party, but everybody invited is able to attend.

Santali shows up with her friend Justin, who shakes Bolton's hand, pats him on the back, and gives him a large bottle of ginger ale. "Santali says you don't drink wine, so I thought...."

"It's perfect, thanks," says Bolton. He takes the extended bottle. "And cold too. Won't need ice."

Paul, Albert, Deena, and Reggie are putting out plates of bacon-wrapped scallop nibbles and mini quiches. Martha is sitting on the couch asking if she can do anything and is being told to sit, eat, and drink. Harold the contractor is there, filling a small plate with canapés before he heads into the kitchen for a bottle of beer.

Genevieve arrives with Trudi, a friend from school whom they introduce to Deena. "You may remember Trudi from the tutorial you conducted for us."

"I do," says Deena. "Good to meet you." She subtly winks at Genevieve, who smiles and blushes a tad, before taking Trudi to meet their mom.

Quelina arrives with Martin, whom she introduces to all. He and Paul air shake hands. "I've heard a lot about you," says Paul. "It's good to finally meet."

"Likewise," says Martin. He holds up a bottle of wine. "I know you don't drink, but I thought a few folks might enjoy a glass."

Paul looks at the bottle. "French. Dry. It's bringing back memories. I'll open it and put it on the kitchen counter, next to the wine glasses. I'm sure it will go, thanks."

Quelina asks Martin if he'll be okay for a moment. Reggie, coming in from the kitchen with more munchies for the table, offers Martin some. "Do you drink beer?" he asks.

"Sure do," says Martin.

Reggie calls into the kitchen, "Hey, Harold, bring out an extra beer."

"I'll need ID," Harold calls back.

Quelina follows Paul into the kitchen. "I just wanted to say, before things really get underway, that we'll start sending you a monthly mortgage check the first of each month."

"He's moving in with you?"

"I'm closest to both our offices, and have the bigger place, so it makes sense."

Paul pours her a glass of wine and hands it to her. He pours himself a glass of mineral water and raises it to her. "Mazel tov!" he says. She toasts him back, smiles, air hugs him, and then rejoins Martin who is talking shop with Harold about renovation projects gone wrong.

Bolton calls everybody to attention. "Find a place to sit folks, or stand behind the couch," he says. "Give me a minute and I'll be back to more formally interrupt your merrymaking." He ducks into his room and comes out with a big box that he puts on the coffee table. He opens the box to reveal a large vanilla-buttered cream-layered cake in the shape of a candle. The cake is covered in psychedelic red, mauve, blue, and yellow icing swirls, looking just like one of Santali's candles. "We are here today to celebrate the sale of Santali's one-thousandth candle."

Everybody applauds and cheers.

"One thousand-plus candles now, all because of a website that Bolton created for me. And..." Santali pauses as Jason hands her a box that he had in a bag he was carrying. She places the box on the coffee table beside her cake. "We are also here to celebrate somebody making a basketball team. She opens the box, which contains a round orange cake with chocolate seams. She lifts the cake and shows it off.

Everybody applauds and cheers as Jason removes the cake box from the table and Santali places the cake on a large platter that Paul has brought in from the kitchen.

"Practices have been going well," says Bolton. "Our first game, an exhibition match against a New York team, is in three days. If I haven't given you a ticket, talk to me tonight. I have freebies."

"But we're not done," says Albert. "Deena has landed several more renovation contracts through the website that Bolton created for her. I believe that makes ten jobs so far? No renovation cake, but lots of renovation money."

"None of which comes from me," says Harold, "and none of which I was in the running for. As I said, there is room for both of us in this business. And just maybe..." He turns to Bolton. "Just maybe I need a website too!"

Everybody applauds and cheers as Deena raises a glass of mineral water in a toast to Albert and then to Harold.

"And I will be speaking at the Canada One entrepreneurial event in about ten days," says Paul. "Which reminds me, I still have to write my freaking talk."

"He's painted it," says Bolton. "I will be in the audience, as I am now a Canada One entrepreneur, and I'm looking forward to seeing how he translates the painting into words."

"Bring it out," Deena says to Paul.

"Nah..."

"Painting! Painting! Painting!" everybody chants.

Paul holds up his hands to calm people down, then turns and limps into his room. Quelina follows him and helps him carry his easel with the canvas on it into the living room. People step back to examine his work.

"Brilliant," says Martin.

"Just because you landed my ex is no reason to butter me up," says Paul with a grin.

"Serious. Love the interplay of the colours," says Martin.

"And the shapes," says Martha.

"It's kind of you, no?" asks Santali.

"Was Bolton speaking to you about that?" asks Paul.

"I see it," says Genevieve. "Abstract, but you."

Suddenly Martha begins to cry.

"Mom?"

"And Mike! My gosh, I can see Mike and his battles. The way he fought. It's like he's still fighting."

Genevieve sits beside her mother and hugs her. Albert sits on the other side and puts an arm around her shoulders. Others hover around the couch.

Martha holds up a hand. "I'll be okay. Once in a while, you know, it hits me. He's gone, but that picture is so him."

Genevieve tightens their hold on their mother. "I miss him too, so much."

"We are all in it," says Deena, as she steps back from the couch. "It's a painting of the four Musketeers. And Mike."

"Paul is the only one of us who can't see it," adds Albert, as he gets up from the couch.

"I'm beginning to," says Paul. "Even more than that, I am seeing my talk in it. I just haven't found the words... But more importantly, we have cake!"

Martha looks up and smiles. "That we do."

"We sure do," adds Santali, coming out of the kitchen with a tray full of paper plates, plastic forks and a large knife. "I hope folks have brought their appetites because we have one heck of a lot of cake to eat."

"There will be doggy bags at the end of the evening!" shouts Bolton to gales of laughter.

Paul and Quelina pull the painting back against a living room wall as people pick up plates and forks. Santali cuts slices of both cakes, putting a slice of each on every plate.

Paul looks at his plate and says, "I know how to eat this." He shoves a forkful of candle cake in his mouth and follows it immediately with a mouthful of basketball cake. He chews, swallows, and then says, "My gosh. If you want to die and go to heaven, try the orange chocolate and the vanilla cake at the same time."

"I guess the Wahl's Protocol diet is still on hold," says Deena with a laugh.

"You think?" says Paul with a grin.

*   *   *

A few days after the party, Bolton takes to the court at the Ryerson arena for his first wheelchair basketball game, an exhibition match against a New York team. Everybody who was at the party is in the stands to cheer him and the team on.

Bolton is guarding New York's best player, Javier Matheson, known for zipping up and down the side of the court and consistently shooting three-pointers from the far corner. Coach Kay told Bolton, "I'm not expecting you to shut him down completely. A solid, able-body player wouldn't be able to do that. But he averages close to thirty points a game. Let's see if you can keep him to under twenty."

By the end of the first half, Javier has only six points, but the Toronto team is behind by twelve. The small but vocal crowd has done its best to boost Toronto's play and Bolton's friends have madly cheered him on, especially when he scores two baskets.

During the half-time break, Coach Kay tells his team that New York has adapted admirably to Toronto's defensive strategy.

"We've all but shut down their best player, he nods at Bolton, but they are using others under the net to two-point peck us to death. He spells out a more offensive plan for his team to implement in the second half. "If we go down, we go down scoring!"

He moves Bolton off Javier and devises methods that he and Jonathan can use to get the ball down the court and pass it off to other players who will be rotating under the basket. Sometimes they'll take a pass and go for a quick layup. Sometimes they'll pass it back to Javier or Bolton in one of the corners of the court for a three-point attempt.

No longer covered by Toronto's fastest player, Javier starts on a hot streak. But once Toronto starts to implement Coach Kay's new system, the team battles back. Unfortunately, the New York lead is just out of reach and Toronto loses by four points.

At the end of the game, in the dressing room, Coach Kay tells his team, "If the game had been seventy-five minutes, instead of sixty, we would have taken them." His players laugh. "Keep your spirits up, boys. We have a lot of games to play before Canada selects its Paralympics basketball team. We keep on playing like we played in the second half today, we'll be in the running."

The players all nod appreciatively and Jonathan shouts, "Go team, go!" Everybody cheers.

After the game, Bolton, his roommates, and most of their friends go out for a drink. There is no talk about where to go, but Harold takes the lead and the others happily follow. Bolton hesitates, but in the excitement, no one notices.

When they are settled around two large tables, hastily shoved together, the waitress arrives to take their orders. The roommates order mineral water or ginger ale.

"Close game. You played well," Paul says loud enough to Bolton so that all those at the tables can hear. Everybody tips glasses in Bolton's direction.

"And we'll play even better our next game," says Bolton as he raises his glass back to cheers.

"You'll show them," Deena calls out as people begin to drink and chat amongst themselves.

Bolton leans in towards Paul, and quietly says, "This is the place."

"The place?" Paul looks around, confused, not sure what the place is.

"Where I got drunk and did cocaine…"

"You should have said something," Paul says in a concerned voice. "There are so many other pubs we could have gone to."

"It's okay. It really is. Kind of full circle, but this time I'm totally sober." He sips his ginger ale. "Full circle. Totally sober."

The two friends clink glasses and raise them to each other in a private toast.

*　　*　　*

A week after the game, it's Paul's day to talk to the entrepreneurs.

Over breakfast, Paul tells his roommates that he's afraid he might be hit by fatigue during his talk. "Taste buds and optic neuritis are fine. Tingles are there, as is the headache, but minimal. Cane combats balance issues, more or less. But fatigue... That's the pain-in-the-butt issue over which I have no control, not that I have control over the other issues. I had a good night's sleep, but think I should try to nap a bit before we head out."

The roommates are empathetic, asking him if there is anything else he should be doing to stave off a fatigue hit. "It's the nature of the illness. You don't know what will happen, when it will happen, or even if it will happen."

A short time later, Quelina shows up. Bolton tells her that Paul is resting. She knocks lightly on Paul's bedroom door. There is no answer. She opens it and peeks in. Paul is lying on his back on the bed, eyes closed She shakes his shoulder lightly. "Fatigue?" she asks.

He yawns and opens his eyes. "Just resting and killing time." She suggests that he get up and get dressed and she'll drive the group to the speaking venue. He agrees. "Beats taking Uber or transit." He rises slowly, sitting at the edge of the bed for a moment, before placing his feet on the floor and reaching out to Quelina to balance himself before he finds his cane.

Thirty minutes later, they all head out the door.

Paul is backstage with Albert, Deena, and Quelina. "Remember," says Albert, "We are here if you need us."

"But need us you won't," says Deena.

"Yoda you speak like," says Paul. Everybody laughs. Paul can hear Nadir on stage addressing the audience and listens for his cue.

"...Now that you all know the breakout room numbers for this afternoon's workshops, that concludes our housekeeping... I'd now like to introduce you to our keynote speaker, Paul Amil, a psychology major from the University of Toronto, a motivational speaker, and a fine painter. His talk today is entitled..." Nadir looks down at his notes. "The Look of Motivation... Without further adieu, Paul Amil..."

Acknowledging the light applause, Paul walks across the stage, using his cane, to the podium. He and Nadir air shake hands and bump elbows to laughter from the audience. Nadir exits. Paul's computer is on the podium. He opens it and presses a key, putting his first of two PowerPoint slides on the screen behind him--a line that he stole from one of his dreams: "Paul Amil is a Fake Motivator."

He clears his throat, takes a sip of water from a glass on the podium, and begins to speak.

"Good morning, entrepreneurs. I am here today to tell you that..." He pauses. "That I am a motivational fraud. I cannot motivate you. It is a lie to say otherwise. I can suggest a couple of things that you might consider doing to motivate yourself, because motivation must come from within. Either you choose to motivate yourself, or you choose not to.

"Having said that, you can sometimes trick yourself, or someone else, into action. For instance, I did not want to do this talk today. I have a friend, an athlete in a wheelchair who is sitting out there with you. I wanted him to try out for the

Paralympics. He said he would, only if I took on this speaking gig. A challenge."

Paul pauses and finds Bolton in the audience. They lock eyes momentarily. "I could only get him to do what I wanted him to do, if I did what he wanted me to do. He is now on the Toronto wheelchair basketball team, competing to make the Paralympics. I am here speaking to you today. We motivated each other." He pauses.

"Or did we?"

Paul sips some water. "If he didn't want to play wheelchair basketball, he would not be playing it. If I did not want to talk, I would not be here speaking today. In other words, we had to trick ourselves into motivating each other to do what we wanted to do all along.

"And that, folks, is where your businesses start. With knowing what you want to do. It can be difficult to figure out what you want to do. It can be even more difficult to do it. We spend much of our lives denying what we want to do, and not doing it, because of fear. Fear of failure and sometimes even fear of success.

"What if I actually try to do what I want to do and fail? That thought, conscious or not, holds us back. In other words, platitudes from me won't motivate you if you don't acknowledge and overcome your fear.

"What if I actually try to do what I want to do and succeed? That thought too can hold us back. Success phobia involves being afraid of achievement for many reasons, sometimes as simple as the fear of change.

"But let me ask you this: What is fear?"

Paul takes another sip of water, places his cane against the podium, and leans forward with his hands holding the podium for support. "It is nothing more than energy. That's what fear is. It is your job to harness your fear, to harness your energy, and to use it to motivate yourself to do what you want to do.

Paul hesitates and takes a breath. "As some of you know, I have multiple sclerosis, or MS. I fear that I might fall over from fatigue part way through my talk today. I had to overcome that fear to be here. I still might fall over. I have no control over that.

But I am no longer afraid of it, because I have three friends backstage who will come out and pick me up if I do fall over.

"To do anything, you have to know what you want to do, you have to overcome fears that might be holding you back, and then you have to do it!

"Take a look at slide two, literally the last slide in today's presentation."

Paul hits a button on his computer. His painting is now on display on the screen behind him.

"You are looking at a self-portrait. And if you don't see me, don't worry. I did not see me at first, either." He takes another sip of water and continues. "I am the red. My MS is the black around me, holding me back. The yellowish colour bleeding through the red? MS symptoms erupting. The blue streaks are my physical, emotional, psychological, and intellectual health working to help me beat back MS.

"No doubt you are asking: 'What does Paul's self-portrait have to do with me?'

"What you want to be, as an entrepreneur, is the red. That means you have figured out what you want to do. MS isn't what is holding you back, but there are elements that can hold you back.

"Fear of failure or success. Do you have enough money to get your business off the ground? Do you have enough time and energy to make your business come together? Do you have a target market? Do you know how to reach them? Do you have competitors?

"Those elements are your dark lines. Your blue streaks are you fighting through those elements. They are you overcoming your fears. They are you begging or borrowing money. Making time or hiring a worker bee to help you. Defining your target market. Determining how best to reach your market. Differentiating your product from your competition and defining its value for your target market. Overcoming your fears.

"Are you saying, 'Are there really so many elements involved in getting my business off the ground?' That is a yellowish symptom boiling to the surface. Use the blue to adjust your attitude, otherwise you might as well find a job, rather than run your own business.

"You have work to do. I cannot motivate you to do it. That can only come from within… And guess what? You might fail. You might fall on your butt! Your so-called MS might knock you down.

"It's up to you to find a way to get back up, dust yourself off, adjust your approach, and try again. You are entrepreneurs. But that means squat if you don't take action. It means squat if you are not prepared to work hard, fail, and try, try, try again.

"I cannot motivate you. I'm just a man with MS who hopes he doesn't fall over while speaking…" Paul pauses and takes a deep breath. "Only you can decide what to do, when, where, why, and how to do it. That is your business."

Paul steps back from the podium. He totters, briefly, but finds his balance. "If any of you think that I am saying you are sick, by comparing you to my MS, know that I am not saying that. I am saying that people who are ill have obstacles to overcome. You too have obstacles to overcome. Only you can identify them. Only you can motivate yourself to overcome them.

"A final word, if I may, about sick people and entrepreneurs. We who are chronically ill, like my friends backstage and my friend in the audience... We have to be entrepreneurial about our lives. We don't fit the nine-to-five work-for-the-boss society. The late, great Stephen Hawking was a fairly sick guy. And I'd put it to you that he was a very entrepreneurial person.

"You folks are entrepreneurs. You don't fit the nine-to-five work-for-a-boss society either. I'm not knocking that society. I'm just saying it's not our society. It's not how our lives are shaped. How do you want to shape your lives? What do you have to do to make your life the shape that you envision it to be?

"Discover who you are. Determine what you want to do. And then find the courage to go forth and do it.

"Thank you for your time. Happy doing."

The applause is resounding. Paul grips the podium with one hand, picks up his cane with the other, bows slightly to the audience and, before turning to leave the stage, leans heavily on his cane.

Paul shuffles backstage, drops his cane, and collapses into the arms of Albert who holds him up as best he can. Deena rushes to help Albert support Paul as Quelina picks up the cane.

"I'll be okay," says Paul in a muffled voice. "Take me home, let me pass out for twenty-four hours, and I'll be fine."

Then his legs give out completely. Albert and Deena bear his weight and keep him on his feet.

As if a sixth sense is telling him that something is amiss, Bolton wheels backstage. He sees Albert and Deena struggling to support Paul and wheels towards them.

"Put him on my lap," Bolton says.

"Say what?" Albert asks.

"On my lap. I can bear the weight. Put one of his arms around my shoulders. You support him on either side and we'll wheel him out."

Gently they seat Paul in Bolton's lap.

"Hold on one second before we move. I want to take his pulse," says Albert. He takes Paul's pulse, which is strong. "He's okay. Exhausted, but okay. Let's go home."

"I love you guys. I really do," mumbles Paul.

"And we love you," says Bolton who breaches post-Covid-19 protocol and hugs Paul, who chokes up a little as Albert starts to wheel them towards the exit.

"That we do," says Albert.

"That we do," echoes Deena who opens a door for the chair to go through.

"Home," waves Paul, his head resting on Bolton's shoulder.

The four friends, moving slowly, head towards the exit. Quelina watches them as they go, Paul's cane in her hands, tears streaming down her cheeks.

Then she remembers that she is their ride home. She wipes away her tears and hurries after them. She can hear them chatting and laughing as they head towards her car in the parking lot. She hears Paul groan, not in pain but facetiously at something that was said. Then he laughs. They all laugh, oblivious to the world around them. The world that too often shuts them out because of how they are. The world that they have learned to ignore, so they can be who they are.

That's who she follows to her car. Four friends who simply are. Despite it all. In spite of it all. They simply are.

Epilogue

Nine months later, Paul Amil is not dreaming. Or he is dreaming about not dreaming? He is not sure. He wakes up, groggy and confused. And then he remembers what day it is…

*   *   *

Paul is at the kitchen table, wearing a new black suit, one that fits decently for an off-the-rack purchase. He's drinking a green-coloured smoothie, mostly spinach with a few other vegetables tossed in.

Deena, in a dark blue dress, joins him. She has a glass of juice. A box of Kleenex is on the table, and Deena reaches over and takes a tissue to dab her eyes. "All I could stomach this morning," Deena says as she raises her glass to Paul.

"I've never seen you in a dress before. You wear it well."

"Been a decade, maybe more, since I had one on." They sit in silence for a moment, and then she asks, "What the heck are you drinking?"

"A Wahl's Protocol breakfast smoothie."

"Does it taste like it looks?"

"Worse. And my taste buds are fine. I'll give the diet three months, assess how I feel, and go from there." Again, they sit in silence for a moment. Then Paul asks in a distracted manner, "How goes the teaching?"

"It's fine. There is a difference between continuing education students and first-year university students. University students are at school for beer, sex, dating, and fun and games. And occasionally grades. Continuing education students, on the other hand, have chosen to take your course at night and want to learn."

Paul chuckles as Bolton wheels up to the table, juice in hand and the kitten, now a young cat, in his lap. He is in a dark grey jacket, one that almost matches his new dark grey loose-fitting track pants.

Paul reaches down and pats the cat. It licks a paw and then rubs its face with it as it begins to purr.

"How do you prepare for a day like today?" Bolton asks.

"You don't," says Deena. "You just take it minute-by-minute, hour-by-hour. Until it's over. And then you go to bed and hope to sleep."

"You have a game tomorrow?" Paul asks Bolton.

"Yes, but I'm not going to play."

"You should. Your options are to sit at home all day doing nothing or sit at home part of the day doing nothing. If you play, I'll come. Besides, you know he'd tell you to play."

"I hadn't thought of it that way. I hadn't really thought it through. We'll see."

"You don't mind if I pass on attending the game?" asks Deena. "I teach tomorrow night, the hammer class. The one he taught last semester. I didn't tell him, but I shot a video on my phone of him as he was teaching. I'm going to connect the phone to the flat screen in the class via the USB port and play it. It's a bit shaky in places, you know how my hands can shake, but overall, it's a decent video of him talking about hammers. He really practiced hard to get it right."

"Are you going to tell the students?" Paul asks.

"I'm not sure. If I don't, for one more night it's not going to feel real. On the other hand, it would be a fitting tribute to him if they knew."

"I'd love to see the video," says Bolton.

"Great idea. We can have a viewing here, for sure," says Deena. She pauses and takes a tissue to blow her nose.

"He had no relatives," Paul says. "His parents were both only children, as was he. They passed away several years ago. No aunts, uncles, or cousins."

"He had us," says Bolton. "And people from the hospital where he worked. I talked to Leon, his friend from before he got sick. He was pretty broken up about it. I gave Leon the information and he said he'd let people at the hospital know."

"I can't believe it was less than a year ago that I collapsed into his arms after my Canada One talk," says Paul. "He was so strong, the way he held me up. And now... It was like somebody snapped their fingers." Paul wipes his eyes with the back of his hand.

"You're going to be okay talking and co-ordinating things?" Bolton asks.

"It feels like that is what I do. Stand and speak, so yeah, I'll be okay." He pulls a piece of paper from his jacket pocket and consults it. "I'll welcome everybody, and then Leon will speak. He asked if he could and I said absolutely. Reggie wants to say a few words as well, so he'll go next."

"They got on famously, worked so well together," says Deena, wiping at her eyes.

"Don't start," Bolton says to her. "Either of you start and I will lose it."

Deena smiles. "I'll be okay until we get there, maybe even okay until Reggie speaks."

The cat leaps off Bolton's lap, finds his water bowl in the corner of the kitchen, and begins to lap at the water.

"After Reggie speaks," says Paul, "I say a few more words, and then you speak, Bolton..."

"If I can."

"And then Deena, the formal eulogy."

"Or I hand my talk to you," Deena says to Paul, "and you deliver it on my behalf."

"You'll do fine," says Bolton.

"I gather he named you executor," Deena says to Paul.

"The will is going to be formally read in a few days at the lawyer's office, but I can give you a synopsis because it's fairly simple. Eliminate all the required legal jargon and it's really a few statements." Paul gets up and pours himself a glass of water to wash down the green smoothie. He sits and takes a sip. "He wanted to be cremated before the funeral, which has been done. He's leaving you, Bolton, one-half of one-third of the rent for two years."

Bolton wipes at his eyes.

"Hey," says Deena, "if I have to keep it together."

Bolton laughs quietly.

"He's leaving a third of what's left to each of the MS Society, Parkinson's Canada, and the Canadian Cancer Society. And that's it."

"Almost," says Bolton "This bit isn't in his will. He gave me the final draft of his novel. I'm going to self-publish it post-humously, which he asked me to do. He wanted me to make the e-book versions available at no cost and the print version at the cost of printing, so there will be no revenue generated from book sales.

"He never talked about it," says Deena. "I respected that and never asked him about it."

"What was it called?" asks Paul.

"You know how your first painting was a group portrait? Well, so was his book," says Bolton. "It's a novel called *Not A Hundred Percent*. Believe it or not, it's a comedy. And it's really funny. But it has touching moments too. Got me tearing up at times. We're not officially in it, but you will see yourselves in the book. I saw me." Bolton wheels over to the fridge and pours himself a bit more juice. He wheels back to the table and says to Paul, "He wondered about using a picture of your self-portrait for the cover."

"I'd be more than honoured," Paul says as his phone beeps. He looks down at the text on his screen. "The car is here. I'll text and tell the driver we'll be five minutes."

"We were four sick people doing as best we could," says Deena.

"And now we are three," says Paul.

"We have just one more thing to do then, before we go," says Bolton. He raises his glass of juice high. "To Albert, an absolutely marvelous, absolutely lovely person!"

Paul and Deena clink Bolton's glass. "To Albert."

As they toast Albert, the cat jumps on the kitchen table, twirls around three times, and sits, looking and the friends, who stare back in silence. The cat licks a paw, wipes his face with it, and begins to purr. The friends break out in laughter, a few tears, and then more laughter.

Then they get up to leave.

Not A Hundred Percent

Albert Booth

Chronic Maladies

Multiple sclerosis (MS) is a disabling disease of the brain and spinal cord (central nervous system). In MS, the immune system attacks the protective sheath (myelin) that covers nerve fibres. This creates lesions and causes communication problems between the brain and the rest of the body, which leads to a variety of symptoms, different for each MS Warrior. Some of the most common symptoms include: fatigue, vision problems, numbness and pins-and-needle tingles, muscle spasms, stiffness and weakness, mobility problems, pain in various parts of the body, cognitive issues or problems with thinking, learning and planning, depression and anxiety. More women than men have MS, but both genders have it.

There is no cure for MS. There are medications that may increase the time between exacerbations and lessen their impact for some MS Warriors. They may also cause negative side effects and may not work for all MS Warriors.

Four MS disease types have been identified:
- Clinically Isolated Syndrome (CIS), or the first MS hit
- Relapsing-Remitting MS (RRMS), in which exacerbations come and go, each hit lasting for a different length of time and of a different severity
- Secondary Progressive MS (SPMS), in which exacerbations come but generally do not go
- Primary Progressive MS (PPMS), the most debilitating form of MS, causes MS Warriors to use canes, then puts them on scooters, then in wheelchairs, and may even cause them to become bedridden.

Parkinson's disease Is caused by a loss of nerve cells in the part of the brain called the substantia nigra. These nerve cells are responsible for producing a chemical called dopamine, a type of neurotransmitter the body makes and the nervous system uses to send messages between nerve cells. This progressive disease of the nervous system is marked by tremors, muscular rigidity, and slow, imprecise movement or difficulty with walking, balance, and coordination. Parkinson's symptoms usually begin gradually and get worse over time.

142

Chronic

As the disease progresses, people may have greater difficulty walking and talking. It chiefly affects middle-aged and older people, but can also affect younger people. More men than women have Parkinson's disease, but both genders have it.

There is no cure for Parkinson's disease, but treatments are available to help relieve the symptoms and maintain quality of life. These treatments include physiotherapy and medications. The medications often lose their effectiveness over time and can cause various side effects.

The five stages of Parkinson's disease include:
- Stage One. Individuals experience mild symptoms that generally do not interfere with daily activities
- Stage Two. Symptoms worsen, including tremors, rigidity, and other movement issues on both sides of the body
- Stage Three. Symptoms worsen in the mid-stage of the disease
- Stage Four. Symptoms are severe and limiting
- Stage Five. Advanced stiffness in the legs can cause freezing upon standing, making it impossible to stand or walk. People in this stage require wheelchairs, and they're often unable to stand on their own without falling.

Paraplegic is a person affected by paralysis of parts of the torso and legs. Paralysis means that muscles in the legs, stomach, back, and possibly also the chest, no longer function. The person affected can no longer walk or stand. Paraplegics no longer feel their legs, but the condition is often accompanied by neuropathic pain due to the spinal cord lesion. People become paraplegic for different reasons. Paraplegia is often due to accidents that cause fractures of the spine Strokes are the most common cause of non-traumatic paraplegia. Genetic disorders, oxygen deprivation, and childbirth complications can also cause paraplegia.

Paraplegics often die as a direct result of their condition. Respiratory failure in cervical lesions and pulmonary embolism in non-cervical lesions are frequent causes of death. Renal failure is also a major cause of death.

As of yet, there is no cure for paraplegia. The paralysis is irreversible, as damaged nerve cells do not regenerate.

Research is ongoing. For instance, researchers at the Mayo Clinic have used a device to electrically stimulate the spines of several paraplegics, allowing them to learn to walk again.

Cancer can be caused by smoking (the biggest cause of cancer and cancer-related deaths), obesity, poor diet, and drinking too much alcohol. Sometimes cancers can have no clear cause and occur randomly. Cancer can be diagnosed at any age, even in children. However, cancer often takes decades to develop, which is why many people are often diagnosed with cancer later in life. Lung cancer is the leading cause of cancer deaths worldwide.

Some people with cancer are treated and go into remission, which indicates that the signs and symptoms of cancer have completely or partially disappeared. Remission can mean that some microscopic, undetectable cancer remains in the body. When cancer returns after a period of remission, it's considered a recurrence. A cancer recurrence happens because, despite the best efforts to rid one of cancer, some cells from the cancer remain and spread. Cancer-free patients are entirely free of cancer.

Cancer treatment options include:
- Surgery to remove the cancerous growth, or as much of it as possible
- Chemotherapy, a drug treatment that uses powerful chemicals to kill cancer cells in the body.
- Radiation therapy, which uses beams of intense energy, often X-rays, to kill cancer cells
- Bone marrow transplant
- Immunotherapy uses certain parts of a person's immune system to fight cancer by stimulating the natural defences of the immune system to make it work harder and attack cancer cells
- Hormone therapy is a treatment that adds, blocks, or removes hormones to slow or stop the growth of cancer cells that need hormones to grow.
- Cryoablation, which uses a needle-like applicator and liquid nitrogen or argon gas to create intense cold to freeze and destroy diseased tissue

About the Author

Based in Toronto, Ontario, Paul Lima (www.paullima.com) has worked as a writer and business-writing instructor for over 35 years. Now retired, he ran a successful freelance writing, copywriting, business writing, and training business since 1988. This is the third novel published under his name. He has also written a collection of short stories and a fourth novel published under a pseudonym. Paul has MS.

Books by Paul Lima:

- *Family Tree: An Historical Novel Spanning 17 Centuries*
- *Chronic: A Sick Novel*
- *Geri: A Post-Pandemic LGBTQ+ Novel About Something*
- *How To Write A Non-Fiction Book in 60 Days*
- *Tell Your Story: How to Write Memoirs and Autobiographies*
- *The Accidental Writer: A Memoir*
- *How to Write Winning Resumes and Cover Letters and Ace Job Interviews*
- *Everything You Need To Know About Multiple Sclerosis*
- *Everything You Wanted to Know About Freelance Writing - Find, Price, Manage Corporate Writing Assignments & Develop Article Ideas and Sell Them to Newspapers and Magazines*
- *Six-Figure Freelancer: How to Find, Price and Manage Corporate Writing Assignments*
- *Business of Freelance Writing: How to Develop Article Ideas and Sell Them to Newspapers and Magazines, Conduct Interviews and Write Article Leads*
- *The Query Letter: How to Sell Article Ideas to Newspapers and Magazines*
- *Produce, Price and Promote Your Self-Published Fiction or Non-fiction Book and eBook*

- *Harness the Business Writing Process: E-mail, Letters, Proposals, Reports, Media Releases, Web Content*
- *Harness the Email Writing Process: How to Become a More Effective and Efficient Email Writer*
- *Fundamentals of Writing: How to Write Articles, Media Releases, Case Studies, Blog Posts and Social Media Content*
- *How to Write Web Copy and Social Media Content*
- *Say it Right: How to Write Speeches and Presentations*
- *Copywriting That Works: Bright ideas to Help You Inform, Persuade, Motivate and Sell!*
- *How to Write Sales Letters and Email: Write direct response marketing material*
- *Unblock Writer's Block: How to face it, deal with it and overcome it*
- *How to Write Media Releases to Promote Your Business, Organization or Event*
- *Are You Ready For Your Interview? How to Prepare for Media Interviews*
- *The Atheist Chronicles: Why the Beliefs of Theists of Every Stripe Are So Unbelievable*
- *Rebel in the Back Seat, Hockey Night On Ossington Avenue, and other short stories*

More information: www.paullima.com/books or email paulmslima@gmail.com.

www.ingramcontent.com/pod-product-compliance
Lightning Source LLC
Chambersburg PA
CBHW031606260626
47154CB00020B/1651